MW01252011

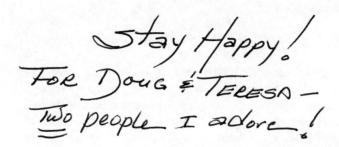

*Stay Happy!*
*For Doug & Teresa —*
*Two people I adore!*

# Of A Predatory Heart

By Joe Parry

*Warmest Wishes —*

*Joe Parry*
*1-'05*

Introduction by Bob Bell

Edited by Kevin Coolidge

ISBN  0-7414-4428-3

*Published by:*

**INFI∞ITY**
PUBLISHING.COM

*1094 New DeHaven Street, Suite 100*
*West Conshohocken, PA 19428-2713*
*Info@buybooksontheweb.com*
*www.buybooksontheweb.com*
*Toll-free  (877) BUY BOOK*
*Local Phone (610) 941-9999*
*Fax  (610) 941-9959*

*Printed in the United States of America*

*Printed on Recycled Paper*

*Published  December 2007*

*For my cherished and beloved family – my wife Linda, my son Justin and daughter Erika, and not to forget my beloved dogs, Bear and Tippy.*

# Contents

Introduction by Bob Bell .................................... 1

Introduction by Kevin Coolidge ......................... 3

Through A Hunter's Window ............................... 5

Song of the Sparrow ......................................... 9

Perfectly Pathetic Predator ............................... 19

A War Baby Doubles ....................................... 31

The Old Timer ............................................... 44

To Cry for Waxwings ...................................... 50

Broken Silence .............................................. 58

The Royal Roachman ....................................... 69

One Man's Fox .............................................. 81

Something About A Gun ................................... 90

Bwana Punda: A Hunter's Love Story ................. 98

One Shot, Thirty-Aught .................................. 109

Roadkills and White-Lies ............................... 121

An Autumn Heart .......................................... 133

Tip's Last Bunny .......................................... 143

A Requiem By Peacemaker .............................. 152

On War & Whitetails ..................................... 165

Of A Predatory Heart .................................... 174

Babbling Tonic ............................................ 183

## Introduction
### by Bob Bell

Joe Parry is an anachronism. He doesn't fit in during the late twentieth century. You can tell that from the things he writes. He still believes in old-fashioned concepts like honesty, human dignity, and doing right even when no one is watching; passing up a small young buck because he earlier decided to concentrate on a gray-muzzled old timer (which means he often goes home at season's end with his rifle unfired); not even thinking of shooting a grouse sitting on a pine limb, because he knows a magnificent game bird like that deserves a better end—one that can be remembered with pride and satisfaction while staring into the dying fire on a cold winter's night with the wind howling through the branches and grains of hard snow rattling against the panes.

He's taught his son, Justin, the same old-fashioned virtues, that some actions are wrong, even when they're not illegal, that a person should have an understanding of the rightness of things. So, Joe found himself largely out of place in today's world, where so many have the attitude "I'm getting mine now, and if you don't—tough." His beliefs have led him down some strange trails, even across the continent, because he thought they might be better found in a younger region where self-reliance was, he hoped, an everyday way of life and hard work brought reasonable reward.

In many ways, perhaps, he was disappointed. But he never changed or gave up hope. You can tell by the stories he writes, that he kept writing through all the years. He usually set them in the outdoors because that is the environment he loves and knows (I almost said milieu, but words like that annoy him; they're too highbrow, too affected, too foreign for his common-man approach) and a natural setting is always important to him, basic, and ultimately essential.

So Joe went on, writing to please himself even when his stories didn't sell, privately screaming at editors who were unwilling to understand what he was trying to do, but refusing to change his view of the world just to suit them. And his perseverance won. For when an occasional story was published, the readers liked them and asked for more ....
Thus this book....

Bob Bell
Mechanicsburg, PA
April 1997

## Introduction
## by Kevin Coolidge

This morning, I wrestled a bear in my pajamas; now, how he got in my pajamas, I'll never know. That's right--I'm from rural Pennsylvania and I grew up loving the woods and the wild things in 'em. I remember fishing for bass with my uncle, and gathering ginseng with my Grandpa and berries with my Grandma (I always ended up with more in my belly than in the basket), and just lying in the backyard under a starry summer sky.

I think modern man has become detached from the land. Sure, he buys and sells it. After all, it's a great investment. They ain't making any more of it. See, the land doesn't belong to man, (and by man, I mean humanity as a whole) it's the other way around. Man belongs to the land, the earth. I believe that the spirit of a place can call to a man. Some folks just belong in certain places. Blood calls to blood and spirit calls to spirit. It sings to you. Draws you in and once it has you in your grasp.... Well, I'm getting ahead of myself again.

I'm writing this introduction for seasoned woodsman, Joe Parry. Joe is just what he appears to be, a blue-collar, working class guy, but Joe has a talent that not everyone has. Joe is a natural story-teller, and he can put it to paper.

The first rule of writing is to write what you know. Joe does one better, he writes what he is, a little guy with a big heart. His stories brought memories of my Grandpa, and my first hunting knife, of that special dog, and some brought tears of laughter. But more importantly, I thought these were stories that would do the same for many people the world over. You know how you read a book so good that you just have to share it?

Yep, this is just such a work. I felt so strongly about it that I edited the work myself and chose to publish it. That wasn't an easy job, since Joe is chock full of tales and has many quality stories. As my Uncle once said, "Give a man a fish and he eats for a day, but teach a man to fish and he'll be drinking beer and spinning tales before you know it."

So, grab a cold drink, hunker down, and enjoy some great outdoor writing.

Kevin Coolidge,
Editor

## "Through A Hunter's Window"

I sit here in my office, more often than not, my indoor sanctuary. A place where feelings and memories come easily, but words come hard. A place where I may brood and think, wonder and dream that which writers often dream. Someone wise once said that even though a writer seems to be merely looking through a window, he is working. And indeed it's true....

The circular moon, that silvery disc upon which flies the sacred Old Glory, placed there by men far braver than I, casts an elongated, abstract likeness; a shadow of an ancient oak tree, now dormant—perhaps sleeping—across the drifted wavelets of snow. Their diminutive peaks so insignificantly, helplessly, reaching for the oceans of the east. Perhaps they were headed there? Where larger, more fluid waters dare to go and, in their frozen, crystallized state, somehow know by some cosmic, celestial Power their effort is, at best futile, in vain? Frozen in their quest. One has to wonder whether there is some universal language, unworldly, known only to wild things, animate or otherwise, who are exclusively worthy of its understanding? Who are we to say? For never in Man's life on Earth will he be as purely innocent as those things of nature found in sylvan glens....

On this night, every star has switched on its porch light, and I sit pondering the hunting seasons past among a multitude of other peaceful, random thoughts and soon come to knowing and feeling a certain sense of prodigious peace; of ever-deepening inner comfort with just the simple knowledge, the threat for them, the whitetails and other wildlife forms has, once again, passed. Like myself, they too are at peace and harm's way is no longer something they must avoid. The dread of winter, their true and worst enemy?

Still, it is not incomprehensible, that one of a predatory nature feels this sense of peace for wildlife? A feeling so ardent, so deep, so strong, it often carves a smile into his weathered face? A hunter? Yes. A man who genuinely and intimately cares for all things wild and free on God's craziest planet? Again, but more definitely, yes!

For as much as I look forward to the hunts, and yes, dread the occasional killing aspect, I embrace more enthusiastically, the end of it all. It makes me warmer in a special place where, not long ago, I felt the painful throes of death. And perhaps does more for that fist-sized muscle than all of Man's most sophisticated surgical procedures could ever manage—and without the scalpel. For once upon a time, a widowed dove sang her plangent, dulcet song for me. Somehow, and strangely, I think I understood.

I feel, sincerely, I have well-earned and am therefore entitled, to the regal title, Hunter. For not only do I think I understand the language of wild things, the needs of all creatures, great and small, but I try wholeheartedly to provide for those needs when indeed, they are the greatest. And I kill only when my ever-aging heart dictates to an ever-aging mind. A mind that shall forever remember that wild places and wild things and wildlife provided this life with its most wondrous moments, sights, sounds, seclusion, and yes, sustenance.

I have been eyewitness to what some less worldly soul may call miracles. Out There. Where miracles happen with each tick of Nature's precious clock; where wonders never cease. Where God and I always walk, my Silent Partner, together...

I have seen the abominable, merciless wrath of Nature, which in no fast or certain way, terminates Life. If

6

something dies by this hunter's hand, it does so cleanly, swiftly, humanely and always with the pain of remorse in my heart…. Always!

I have wept watching the white-tailed fawn's birthings in springtime and done the same, only with increased emotion, as through glistening eyes, I observed the deer of the winter yards dying from starvation; their skins stretched heinously over their fragile ribcages like the hides on snare drums. And yes, it is always the young of the herd to perish first, without pity from their elders. As in only the strong survive. As in we eat first and you my little one must die.

I have had chipmunks wriggle up the no-no end of my double shotgun then back out quizzically and comically. Gray squirrels have perched upon my sun drenched shoulders in the warmth of the autumnal sun and once, one jumped as high in the air as God and Nature, one in the same, might allow when I whispered a simple, "Good mornin,' little one!" And I've had whitetails so close the funneling steam from their flared nostrils fogged my shooting glasses and I could smell the cud of vegetation on their breath.

I've cried at the death of a cedar waxwing who succumbed after my desperate efforts to heal her wounds failed. And there was a time not too long ago when I smiled with a certain confidence in my hunting heart as a most heavily antlered white-tailed buck was allowed to walk past my morning stand—within twenty yards—knowing his life was purely at the mercy of my sentiment at the moment. He did not die by my hand. Me, the lover of the sacred, ritualistic buck hunt? Yes! Why did I not end his life, this once-in-a-lifetime-buck, so elegant and furtive, perhaps that morning making his greatest mistake? I don't know….

And commonly, I've had black-capped chickadees tiptoe onto my cap as I sat beneath protective hemlocks. Ever so gently then, onto a shoulder. How often I've asked a mutual God to let me in on just what, exactly, they were thinking as, again, I whispered my startling, notorious, "Good mornin,' little one!" He never has. Yet…

Sylvan magic, wildlife wonders, miracles in the making? Abundant and available to the hunter. The seeker of miraculous sights, sounds and wild songs...

Perhaps someday, God will let me in on the secret, magical language of wild things? Perhaps He'll say, "Okay, here's what the chickadees said those times they lit upon your shoulder..." And then again, maybe not? I suppose this is why I'm a hunter. A keeper of wild places. A vagabond of pine-thick meadows. That way, when he does begin to teach me, On High, I'll have a great advantage to understanding it all. Finally.

Right now, a predaceous intuition prods me to look out to the field across the road. I see ebony silhouettes of five, strung-out white-tailed deer. They glide silently like the shadows of nightly clouds in the cast light of the full moon; against the very Mother who gave them Life.

Perhaps they'll succumb to the elements, the wrath? I pray not. Perhaps they'll make it into springtime, finding renewed life in verdant meadows? I pray so...

For it is these living miracles, in no small way, that brought my hunting heart to the profound realization that I hunt not so much to kill, but to more intimately learn the true value of life; to further drive home to the heart, the precious nature of it all and thus, be grateful.

As a hunter, a sort of paladin of all things wild and free, I will pray on this starry night. That the time I'm allotted between this moment and the day I'm taught the Tongue of the Wild is long. With many nights of beautiful, silvery moons and whitetails silhouetted against a steel blue, wintry sky. For these are memories able to sustain me. Surely, you understand why?

Dedicated to "Bear", my dog, my life's most marvelous friend and in so many, many ways, the absolute love of my life—64 years of it. Rest "Bear". Rest...

Love You,
"Pop"

Many veterans of war, from the 19th-century until the current Iraq war, come home lacking the desire to ever kill again, if just for a while or for a lifetime. Some teeter back and forth in their desire to hunt, which is the case of the veteran in this story as it was for his father in the piece, "On War & White-tails." This is for vets everywhere who have endured the pains of war and come home to find peace in their lives, to sort things out and hopefully, hunt once again if indeed they hunted prior to their involvement over "there." And certainly, this is for those who never made it home. You will never be forgotten and the world must surely hope you've gone to a better place…JMP

## "Song of the Sparrow"

Everyone who hunts or has hunted vividly remembers that first kill, first gun, and first dose of the always familiar remorse. Feelings and tastes are bittersweet in nature for the hunter. Almost every hunter's first kill is a bird – and not usually a game bird. The first gun is often times a Daisy lever-action. A formidable .177 caliber…

The first disheartening, wrongful kill, quite often is a sparrow. Perhaps, in an excited state— a state quite natural for the hunter to be – after receiving the deadly Daisy, he may slither, Indian-like, through a grove of spruce, a youngster playing soldier, bellied to the ground as if he were avoiding unfriendly fire. Stalking, he slides atop the slippery, needled ground, first using his ears to hone in on the song of the sparrow. Then, seeing the flitting, mottled chirper upon a bough of spruce, his instincts kick in and he chambers a coppered round and aims, ever so carefully. He fires and hears for the first time, the unmistakable and hollow thud of a hit. With the warm, dead sparrow in his hand, he learns how quickly remorse breeds. In an instant he learns of bittersweet and it will leave an indelible etching upon his heart. It is necessary, this lesson, even though it hurts him...

The man in this story found his first gun beneath a Christmas tree, and his first kill went much like that explained here. The gun was a Daisy; the kill, a sparrow. The gun he no longer has but the sorrow of that wrongful kill lingers, still today. There's a chamber in a man's heart that hangs on to these things. And never, but never, allows them to leave. Nature's way perhaps of reminding him to refrain in the future? Of giving him something to think about, evaluate, and, ultimately, determine whether in fact, he is truly a hunter? In most cases he learns that he is and thus matures into someone more responsible, more dignified, more selective, and legal with regard to his various pursuits afield. It doesn't come upon him like a bolt of lightning. But more so like the Chinook Winds; subtle, yet impactful and powerful like that of water dripping constantly onto a rock. Eventually, it leaves a mark which, through time, grows deeper.

His hunting objectives change as years leave him and those things he once so needed to accomplish become less important. In his twilight years he will have arrived at a place he never knew existed. Perhaps, not so much a place, but instead, a time. A time in his life which will afford him an understanding of it all. The need to stalk and hunt and kill. His memories of hunts past and fallen prey and frustrating, fruitless days, as well as those days when everything flew just right or ran broadside at close range, will be as clear to him as the summoning bells of Notre Dame Cathedral.

He may realize a distinct sadness if and when he no longer feels the atavistic urge to hunt, and he may reluctantly forego everything the autumn woods once provided him. Though, in his mind and heart, he will hunt until he dies.

And all of this began with a vintage '52 Daisy air rifle and the sweet song of a sparrow, long dead.

This man has kept, for forty-four years, since that day of the sparrow, a backyard feeder well stocked, for all birds, a chore of passion in memory of his wrongful kill of '52. For that fallen sparrow had taught him, among many things, that indeed it is more important how a man lives than how he dies; of reverence for wild things; of undiluted hatred for wanton waste.

Time in the fields and woods almost demands that a hunter become more sophisticated – a maestro, a collector of tack-driving rifles, smooth-swinging shotguns, and crystal-clear optics. It all stems, perhaps, from his desire to realize near-perfection. In his furtiveness, yes, but more in his penchant for instant kills. He is completing a circle of sorts. One which will hopefully end with him in an oaken rocking chair with a store of sweet memories to ponder. Memories that will serve him well and fill him as needed. And, save for the fallen sparrow of 1952, clean as the driven snows of November.

And just as this young hunter neared the peak of his prowess, his expertise, his sophistication in the hunting fields, a war in the jungles of Asia beckons him, and not being a Flower Child, draft-card burner, or a van driver with a head full of highly intoxicating smoke and a belly full of vegetables and hard liquor, he goes. Not gladly, but not reluctantly either. His father provided him this quality, these values, this love of country – right or wrong with regard to their involvement or quest.

The land there in the jungles was strange to him, at best; frightening as it swallowed him easily as might the whale of fame in the classic, "Moby Dick." The snakes alone were capable of stopping a man's heart within minutes of the accurate strike. The blood-sucking leeches deprived him the feeling of cleanliness, which, as his mother always chimed, "...was next to Godliness." The rains, there called monsoons, drenched not only land, but spirit, that normally happy spirit of G.I's not so engaged. He seemed a captive to this strange jungle, the deadly killers that not only slithered but those others, those unseen enemies which shot from trees or impenetrable foliage; the hidden pits in the jungle's floor.

He was forever glad he was a hunter that he could handle a rifle, that he was able to attune himself to the wildness of strange places and that he could, if he wanted and needed, kill-instinctively or otherwise. Glad was he that his senses were sharp as that of his carbon steel bayonet, that he was keenly aware of those things around him he needed to avoid if he was to survive. He felt primitive, savage but confident that he would work his way out of all this jungle madness, and often summoned soporific memories of swamp pheasants, bottomland white-tails and grape-tangle grouse. Even though in the chaos of it all, those memories were at times of a tenuous nature. Still, it was his way of retaining sanity and dissolving fear. All of these things were now but fantasies, dreams he wanted to once again realize; yet, he knew. Knew deep down, he may never again see a white-tail, hear the thunder of a grouse, or awe at the autumnal beauty of a hickory-laden hollow...

He remembered his father's frequent words. "You kill it, son, you eat it." His father neglected to mention war; the killing of men. And his first three kills in combat were at close range, that distinct hollow sound of a hit once again stinging his ears, several hits...Those VC fell but ten feet from the muzzle of his rifle and strangely, all he thought of at the time was the little fallen sparrow, that long ago sorrowful misdeed, in the spruce grove. He thought daily, "I may never hunt again, even if I live through all of this." But his God saw to it that he did, at least, get home.

There were no parades, no banners, no flag-wavers to welcome him back. But he was grateful that there wasn't a VC, a Charley behind every tree, and that was reward enough. And the hunter inside of him began to awaken. He walked in the woods and smiled with a certain familiarity he felt. His swamp and woods were his official greeters and nothing there seemed to have changed, nothing there was superficial, unnatural or frightening. Back then and now, he felt his heart flutter with the evening call of a rooster pheasant. "Nature's rendition of Taps," he thought aloud. And he headed home…

He wondered if he would or could hunt again. The jungle had taken an unseen toll upon his heart and way of thinking with regard to killing. "For man to kill man is not." He was startled out of his meditative mood by a stabbing in his back, a pain he'd carried from the jungle in the form of shrapnel un-removed.

Small game season came shortly after he'd gotten home and his childish level of anxiety seemed intact and it felt as wonderful as always. He felt ready, excited and hopeful. He walked to the hardwoods below his mountain home where he planned a grouse or two for the evening meal. Perhaps a few gray squirrels. He wasn't sure, he didn't really care, and it never did matter all that much to him. He hunted mostly to capture feelings, create memories, and lighten his heart. A heart that now needed lightening more than ever before. The killing had always been, to his mind and heart, largely beside the point. And always, things out there seemed to fall into just the right places. As Nature and God, one entity, wanted it. And he always felt like an actor, merely playing out a role, working a cosmic script, written for him the day he was born.

This first day back in the hunting woods afforded him ten chances to kill – seven grays, three ruffed grouse. But his game bag at dusk was empty. Something had happened to him and even though the sights and sounds of the day filled him, he was overcome with his decisions not to kill. The confusion was cumbersome, perplexing, and he was unable to answer his very own question, a simple "why?" Then he thought of old Chief Joseph of the Nez Perce Tribe. And to himself he said, "I may kill no more, forever?" He thought of the Asian jungles, the fallen sparrow, and though he hadn't died in that faraway land and had come home as he prayed, his hunter's heart was dying right here at home. His freezer remained devoid of small game…

Deer Season: And the winds of autumn carried the pungent smells of decaying forest litter; exciting smells always. The phone sounded and his friend's excited voice said,

"Hey, Partner! How's it goin'? Time to pack the camp duffel and fill your pockets all with snoose tins!"

"Naw, not this year, Oz. I think I'll just stay here at home and maybe hunt around here."

His friend pleaded, "C'mon, you big sissy, let's get it together and head for camp!"

It wasn't to be. His winter was spent reading the literary works of Gassett, Ruark, Hill, Waterman, O'Conner, and Thoreau. Trying somewhat to fantasize, but it didn't work for him. It didn't carry even one of the joys he thought it might; hundreds of pages of reading…

His racked guns carried the dusts of wintertime, forced-air heat. He spent a winter without his sacred venison, without savory memories and with few phone calls from hunting friends. Silence was the tongue, the language of his empty heart and there was a tenuous nature about his choices; those being to forego the ritualistic charm of it all, the camp stay, the deer hunt. For somehow, the melody of the deer-hunting process, of the hunting process in general, was no longer stentorian insofar as reeling him in…

Springtime brought the incessant, raspy chorus of high, chevroned Canadian Geese; the songs of the creeks returned to the hollows near his home, and the now chilling rains caused the marsh peepers to chorus their way through the nights. The pallid meadows allowed the rains to color in their character, nourish their wildflowers, and make feed for winter-thinned whitetails. The whole of the home-front geography went into a splendiferous metamorphosis, and his heart seemed, once again, alive and full and glad to be pounding within his chest – the pagan emptiness gone for now.

Then summer brought ever-thickening clover and woodchucks to the fields near his home – countless woodchucks, forever bobbing nervously and tentatively about the meadows abundant with wild forbs and flowers. The doves, long back on summer nesting grounds, were now slightly imprinted and graciously sang their seemingly mournful songs for him from nearby wire-strand perches, somehow soothing the heart of the former hunter—former soldier...

Sitting on the redwood deck of his pedestrian home one early morning, enjoying the unfolding of it all and an authoritative mug of ebony-colored coffee, he spotted his longtime friend, Oz, speeding up the long, dusty drive. "Oz Andretti!" he thought, "Wonder what he's doing here so early?"

Oz slid to an abrupt, dusty stop and was out of the Subaru wagon before it had stopped completely. He opened the hatch, beating the settling dust and without so much as a greeting such as "Hello, Buddy", Oz yelled to him, "Hey Partner! Look at this baby!"

Oz handed him a rifle not a whole lot smaller than an anti-tank bazooka of WWII vintage. "It's a Ruger, bull-barreled, two-twenty Swift and very d-e-a-d-l-y!"

"Oz, my father attached vent pipes to the tops of water heaters that were smaller than the tube on that thing! Why in God's world would you want that thing?"

"Got any chucks out there at 300-yards, I'll show ya, little buddy!"

"Lottsa chucks, Oz, but how in the world are you gonna hold that beast steady, offhand?"

"Ya don't, Dummy, look at this!" Oz went to the open hatch and came out with a tripod, and, planting it into the yard sod, said, "C'mon, look through the scope. I have it on twelve power."

Looking through the crystalline optic, he spotted a woodchuck. "There's one, Oz! Go ahead, take a shot at it, show me how good you are with that cannon!"

"Me? You shoot it, that's why I brought it over, for you to try!"

"Oz, I ain't trying nothing. Nothing..."

Oz offered, "Well at least line the little porker up in the scope, fer cryin' out loud. What's that gonna hurt?"

He lay behind the rifle, peered through the scope and asked, "How far do ya figure that chuck's out there, Oz?"

"'bout three hundred, I'd say, give or take."

"Where would a guy hold on a shot that far with this howitzer?"

"Right where you want the bullet to impact, my friend."

"Really? It'll be right on that far out?"

"Bet your sweet bippy, buddy. That's a Ruger Swift, one fine combo, period!"

The former hunter could feel his pulse accelerate, his primordial instincts kicking back in to that place within, where they always had been, however dormant.

"Right on, huh?"

"Yep. Wherever you want the bullet to be. Think the range is about three hundred, maybe a little better, Oz?"

"Yep. I do, how about you?"

"I think you may be real close, Oz, real close!"

The Ruger sounded and Oz, somewhat surprised, squinted as he looked out into the heat waves of the summer field.

Well?" Oz questioned. "How'd ya like it?"

"Fine piece of weaponry, I'd say, and there's no doubt, that old chuck never knew what hit him! This is some rifle, my friend."

And the hunter was "back." Something deep inside of him blossomed once again, torched his love of the hunting challenge. Just as he'd hoped, deep down, would one day happen.

Still today, he has some annoyance with the killing. But, back in the early 1980's, he became a full-time, freelance outdoor writer, and so he kills, and hunts, and stalks, and fishes, forever making personal choices, selective always, during each of his pursuits. And although he's given up certain forms of the hunting he so loves, he celebrates the caring hunter supportively.

He knows the instincts deeply imbedded won't be easily dispelled, and he knows, too, that killing is a means by which wild things are kept in favorable balance and he feels good about his choices in the autumn fields. He knows his bullets will consistently fly true and kill quickly—far more merciful than time.

He feels good about not leaving the hunting to those who care less than he and too, feels deep in his heart, that, if given a choice, game animals, if indeed they could understand and choose, would opt for the swiftness of the hunter's bullet rather than the many, and uglier, alternatives.

He ponders that long-ago, albeit distasteful, lesson he learned from the fallen sparrow. And he is happy knowing he "heard" and listened to her ancient, last song, understanding that he'd made a terrible mistake. For over the years that followed, he made up for his error in judgment a thousand-fold by doing that which is right, and biologically sound, in the hunting fields.

Perhaps, if there weren't seemingly mindless hunters-to-be out there, to make that single, remorseful mistake with an indiscriminate Daisy air rifle, there simply wouldn't exist the sweet, melancholy songs of sparrows? He believes that today, but didn't back then, when the bitterness of the kill seemed so ugly, so pungent to his tastes, so hurtful to his young, then innocent heart. To him, killing in the autumn fields is like the dreaded tetanus injection for preventing locked jaws. He knows it will hurt, but too, knows it is necessary.

He feels that as long as we the hunters, forever listen to the songs of the sparrows, the language of wild tongues, we will always do that which is correct, righteous, with regard to conduct in the hunts of tomorrow and throughout our lives. For never in the annals of wildlife history, have sparrows been known to mislead, lie, or sing a deceptive song, never. And yes, at least one sparrow, long gone, but not forgotten, brought the hunter in this story back to that place he wanted to be all along. Just a single, precious little sparrow, imagine…

Late summer, his wife stepped outside onto the deck where he sat jotting notes for a story. Glancing over his shoulder, he questioned, "What's for supper, Sweet Pea?"

She pushed his cap down over his eyes and said, "I saw you had something thawing on the kitchen counter, so I didn't bother to take out anything! What is that you have thawing?"

"Woodchuck", he answered, "We're having southern-fried and very tender woodchuck."

"If we're having woodchuck, Bwana, you're doing the cooking!"

"Not a problem," he said; "I wouldn't have it any other way. I was merely waiting to see whether you'd taken something from the freezer I didn't know about." He continued jotting notes and whistling his haunting tune.

His wife, now inside, yelled out, "What's that song you're whistling?"

"Don't really have a name for it, why do you ask?"

"Well, it's very pretty. Do you know the lyrics?"

"Not really, Sweet Pea, only the meaning."

"Okay then, Mr. Whistler, what is the meaning?"

"Means we're gonna have venison this winter."

Again, his wife questioned. "Where did you learn the song?"

"Oh, from a little sparrow, a long, long time ago, not only taught me the tune, but something far more important about life and death, I doubt I'll ever forget…"

Author's note:
It somehow feels important and pertinent to note that the hunter in this story skinned and ate every woodchuck he killed that summer and every summer thereafter. He tanned the hides with the hair on and used them, stitched together, to cover the interior walls of his loading and fly-tying shanty; as a sort of poor man's insulation. The tails of the chucks are used in several of his fly patterns-and the feet? He dehydrated those, made a hole in each in order that they could attach to a strand of rawhide which made, he says, "…for an eerie looking necklace." At Halloween, he handed these out to Trick & Treating children of the neighborhood along with, of course, a generous handful of hickory-smoked jerky. No wanton waste in this hunter's life…

18

"Perfectly Pathetic Predator"


"Just look at your pitiful self! Why you're without doubt the most pathetic specimen of desirability I've ever seen! To think I married you and had the courage to hang in there for twenty-three years! Had I known you'd eventually flip your lid, why. . ." The words of a loving wife?

Yes. But I stood there, unmoved by her callous outburst, as a monument of sheer masculinity, before her in my most recent, rather small, investment. One that cost little more than the furniture in our living room. **The** investment which cost me a mere 18% APR interest for a paltry two years? **The** complete battle array of a real-life Orion the Hunter. The lavish, deceiving garb of the archer which, to my simple mind, made me symbolic of the ultimate male— even though my loving wife had suddenly become a current day Artemis. But then, she's the same gal who thought monogamy was a type of wood....

My hair was packed and slicked down with a rather pungent mixture of top soil and clay. Protruding from this concoction I'd extracted from the breast of Mother Earth were branches of mountain laurel with just the right touch of multi-flora rose stems for the total effect. These would surely add to the most natural guise even though they were a bit on the aggressive side.

My face was splendiferous in its coats of green, black and brown and very greasy theatrical makeup. Leaving just the whites of my eyes to reveal what actually lay behind this disguise—the confident sneer of the ultimate predator. There would have been more had I been able to get something that would adhere to my eyeball whites, but no. They were simply too moist.

My neck wore a goodly amount of the same makeup and this natural blending carried well down into my chest area. Just in case it got hot in Yonder Wood and I was forced by discomfort to open my first few shirt buttons. I left no stone unturned.

My shirt was of a common camouflage. Leafy pattern to be sure, but I thought it cunningly strategic to staple on a number of real oak leaves, again, for the natural effect. According to my cajoling wife, "You look like the grand marshal of the National Arbor Day parade!" Perhaps. But I was soundly content with the fact and certain knowledge that I would sooner or later send forth a killing arrow into the vitals of a white-tailed buck.

Britches matched the shirt pretty much. But the belt I'd fashioned from wild-grape vine concerned me a touch, perhaps because I felt it contrasted too much with everything else? I felt I could live with that if the deer would and so, I kept it wet and viable for the intended purpose—to hold up my pants. I did, for the sake of those newer to the sport, find tying a knot in the vine rather difficult and a bow with loops is totally out of the question!

My boots were a remnant of Vietnam war days. Half camo on the upper part, and leather on the bottom. I pondered that shiny, black leather area for the longest time, thinking whitetails are much smarter than Charley (VC) was and finally decided to have my wife tackle and solve the problem for me. "Honey! Would you please sew me a couple of booties out of that green blouse material you bought to slip over my boots?" That completed, I had her tack on two slab-like sections of old, worn-out snow tire I'd found in the garage. Cut to my size, I told her, "Sweetheart, if I'm gonna be a furtive archer, I'd best have good and quiet traction material on my feet!" Enter a snicker here from someone's wife. . .

My hands were concealed with two green rubber gloves I'd salvaged from under our kitchen sink. Upon these, I painted a matching leaf pattern and went so far as to paint on several acorns in burnt tan; and complete those with little acorn nut caps. No sir! **No** stone unturned. . .

Ah yes, my bow! A thing of high-tech beauty to say the very least. This thing has more wheels than a garbage truck and more lines here and there than I cared to count. They crisscrossed and reminded me very much of my Interstate highway map. Attached to this one cord were two little rubber ditties that looked like a species of Arachnid – or spider, for the sake of those not biologically inclined. To the avid bass anglers? They resemble jig skirting. Whatever, these constantly-dancing little items function (so I was told!) as string silencers and at the start I felt they should be sold by the dozen what with cords crisscrossing every which way. As I approached my wife with the aggressive little things she goes haywire even though I tell her, "They're absolutely harmless, Sweetheart!"

"You're **totally** pathetic!" She squealed as she ran from the kitchen. "I swear, **absolutely** pathetic!" Obvious now where I got the story title?

My sights are of the pin variety, the tips of which are painted in brilliant fluorescent colors. These too, at first were, confusing due to the fact that the low pin is used for higher arc or longer distance while the high pin is used for lower arc and shorter distance. Initially, I assumed (hate that word!) the middle one to be a Come-What-May-And-Hope-For-The-Best sight-pin?

I worried not, however. I'd practiced shooting in my back yard for months on end. I just hoped my neighbor, Clyde, didn't ruin his new lawn mower when he shredded all the stray arrows that sneaked into the root system of his yard. Arrows that completely defied detection as though they were "alive," furtive and hiding! Nonetheless, there were a couple of dozen. If Clyde should find them? I tried consoling him with, "Just be careful Clyde, old buddy. They ought to surface with the spring thaw and new grass growth!"

A further attempt at comforting my worried neighbor. "Clyde, it could be much worse, ya know? Just thank your lucky stars they weren't razored broadheads. I know how you enjoy working barefooted in your yard!" Clyde didn't find that funny and I never got a smile for the verbal effort so, I added the following to determine whether Clyde still retained his usual and simple sense of humor. "Why, you tramp on a broadhead with your bare little tootsies and you'd have to call yourself a "toe" truck, old buddy!" Nothing from Clyde. "Get it, Clyde? Toe truck? T-O-E truck?" It didn't work. Clyde just wasn't smiling, but he did manage to ask whether my life insurance was current. And I'm relatively certain he wasn't asking so he could help me pay the monthly premium. . .

In the house, my usually intellectual wife, a former school teacher, asked, "Who's the broad with the nice head you and Clyde were speaking of?" I declined explanation as, at the moment, I could clearly hear Clyde screaming.

"I ain't had a lucky star since you moved into the neighborhood, Robin Hood!" Good old Clyde, witty as always.

Now then, back to my stuff. My quiver was of the quicky-type about which my wife made snide remarks. Granted, when I initially saw how this outfit who makes the quiver spelled quicky, I was a bit skeptical with regard to the intellect of archers. Apparently it didn't run rampant in "our" ranks? Quicky being spelled, K-w-i-k-e-e. Regardless, it too was decorated well in camo paint and securely held the arrows in place.

I positioned the release/trigger mechanism in the nocking area and my loving wife came up with yet another comment. "Boy, you'll need that!" She said as I explained its function, "You're not nimble-fingered enough to button your own shirts, let alone hold that skinny little arrow in place!" I told myself to just ignore such mistaken perceptions regardless of how close to the truth they were, and went on about my business.

All in all, excluding the abundant labors of my loving spouse, with the possible total destruction of Clyde's lawn mower, practice time of several hundred hours and driving time to scout faraway scrapes and potential stand locations, I had about $1,395 wrapped up in my stuff—give or take a few (okay 10 or 12!) twenty-dollar bills. But, I was ready! The hay bales holding my targets were reduced to mere piles of fine alfalfa grain in the back yard. One thing, however, remained bothersome to me, being the type who deplores loose ends. The loose ends in this case being in the form of some 9 or 10 target arrows protruding from Clyde's dormer.

For love nor money, I couldn't figure a way to get to them without getting caught. And I doubt Clyde would ever have noticed had most of the starlings in the neighborhood not taken a liking to them, using them more often than not as an early morning and late afternoon perch! Clyde developed this terribly negative attitude about the cute little birds just because they whitewashed an entire side of his house. The perches, of course, making this habit of theirs rather convenient and those directly above Clyde's back door seemed especially annoying as it seems the host of birds ruined two of Clyde's favorite hats, not to mention his boss's 20X Stetson that got "decorated" one morning. Clyde's language and threats may have gotten him into serious trouble that day with the National Audubon Society. Lucky for him, shooting within the town limits is illegal (for me too, according to Clyde!).

Opening day found me in my stand well before daylight. It was raining, but I enjoy hunting in the rain since it drives scent into the ground; however, it is tough on makeup format. Most of mine left my face, ran down my neck front and back, then down my chest and stomach, neatly depositing itself in a marble-like mixture in the depths of my belly button and, not having any lint in there to absorb some of the runoff, it continued downward. It goes without saying where that makeup ended up as it cascaded down the

23

back side. But no matter, I was hunting and happier than a pig in slop. . .

About an hour into the hunt, the first deer appeared. All alone, this plump little six-pointer (eastern count) and my arrow was nocked and ready. I drew it to my cheek, held steady and the whisper of the speeding arrow barely broke the silence of the drizzly morning. At least until that arrow and three others I shot slammed into a tree some 15-feet behind the little buck. He simply milled around, then headed off into the bush. If I correctly recall, all four shots were taken with the "Come-What-May-Pin?" Obviously, the wrong one!

About another two hours had passed when I noticed five deer picking their way into the same shooting "lane." Same smooth draw this time, good hold then, "pssst" went the broadhead through the forgiving air, then "kerplunk," into the ground some 10-feet in front of the troop of deer. They were out of there in a hurry with the 8-point leading! I was totally bewildered and aloud I thought, "Must be all these sight pins are of the come-what-may variety?" I took an "Oh Well" attitude, knowing there were plenty of deer out there and they were seemingly active. I just prayed that at least one buck was less intelligent than I. Fat chance?

After lunch, I settled in again. After a short time waiting, lo and behold another buck, a loner, nosing his way right toward me, apparently winded my doe-in-heat scent, though his curiosity could have been triggered by the fact that I'd drenched my attire in the stench of rotting apples for several weeks in the confines of a black garbage bag? Whatever, he was coming! Hell-bent for amorous activity which, at the moment, made me thankful I was off the ground and in the tree! His head down, seemingly unaware of my presence, I thought, "Just one thing on that Romeo's mind." I slid the arrow across the rest and to my cheek. The release felt good as the arrow sliced its way through the rain, then "choonk!" A hit! The buck hunched up then bolted for cover; however, just seconds after he'd gone, I heard him pile up not too far away. I knew he was down and dead, for the arrow had buried itself to the fletchings just behind the right shoulder.

I left my bow aboard the shooting platform of the stand and in my haste to get to the buck, I fell some 15-feet to the ground (where else?) buttocks down! The imprint of said incident remains there today!

Sitting there rather stunned, I heard, then saw another hunter coming my way. With no time to compose myself or position my body into other than the sprawling manner in which it was, I hurriedly grabbed a granola bar from my shirt pocket with the hope he'd believe I was merely having a relaxing snack. "Mornin'," I said, "just figured I'd have me a relaxin' snack here. Little bite t'eat for energy, right?"

The hunter, half smiling asked, "Izzat your buck I just passed over yonder?"

"Yep, he's mine alright! Just figured I'd have me a bite before the chores." I said, chuckling, "Heh, heh. . ."

"Mister," he said, "you must be awful dadgummed hungry cause I hain't never seen **anyone** come out of a tree quite that fast!" He then walked away, lengthening the distance between us when I heard him holler. "Hey! There's several arrows in this here tree over here! They yours?"

"Yeah! Yeah, they are!" I answered red-faced.

He bellowed back, "Nice group but ya oughtta do your practicing at home!"

I yelled back at him, "Thanks! I'll remember that!" Somehow I don't think he heard me over his raucous laughter.

I cleaned up the buck, made my usual sacrificial offering to the hunting gods, took him to the truck and loaded him for the trip home. I drove literally awash in ecstasy having found this new (to me) and exciting method of hunting and being successful first time out. Orion, I thought, eat your heart out, buddy!

Clyde saw me pulling into the drive (he **always** did!) and my buck was highly visible through the open tailgate. Immediately, he ran into his garage. I felt, perhaps, he was envious of my proficiency with the complicated compound.

Into the house I went, happier than an osprey at a sushi party!

"Hi Honey, I'm home!" Apparently she'd seen my buck protruding from the truck and it didn't impress her? I soon learned I was in direct competition with Robert Redford in a TV movie so, needless to say who lost the battle for my wife's undivided attention. I always wondered why women liked a guy with surfer-like hair and moles, but so be it. On his cheeks yet! Sure, he's pretty, but who wants a pretty man? Most women, that's who!

She did find the decency to acknowledge my being alive at least, since she saw the buck from the living room window, "Just get the poor thing to the processor before it spoils!" That was all she said. No generous congratulations or "atta boys." Nothing! Which brings you to a clear understanding of my undiluted hatred for Redford! I'd been walking in his shadow for too many years now.

Outside, I could hear Clyde. He'd busied himself with feverish, incessant pounding, nailing what appeared to me to be sheet metal panels to his dormer. "Whatchya doin' there, good neighbor? Did ya get a gander at the buck I arrowed?"

"Yeah, yeah, I saw it! Which is precisely the reason I'm protecting this dormer with heavy gauge sheet metal! I just know darn good and well you're gonna be back at it again next fall after getting that buck and this here metal ought to serve as good protection against your many stray arrows. And right now, I'm hopin' some of them eventually glance back toward you!" Good old Clyde, loves to joke.

I picked up the wrapped venison the following morning. When I brought it into the house, my wife asked, "How much venison in the little box, Tonto?" This reference to a good Native American, one Jay Silverheels, I felt was due to my archery expertise. But I should have known better.
. .

"Thirty-eight pounds, Sweetheart!" Budget-minded as she always is, she whipped out her trusty calculator from the pocket of her apron so fast it would have embarrassed Pat

Garret or Wyatt Earp, then went into statistics at about Mach 1!

"Let's see now, you put about $1,395 on our credit card for all your archery junk, right?"

"Yes, Dear. Gee, your hair looks marvelous today!"

"Never mind that!" she snapped. "Okay, thirty-eight into one-thousand, three-hundred and ninety-five dollars, right?"

"I think so, Sweetie?"

"Well, Tonto, that comes to $36.71 per pound we have invested in that meat!"

Defensively, I came back with, "Yes, but ya can't buy the stuff. So what then is it worth? Stuff is priceless, that's what!"

"Look buddy," she said staring at me like I was a known felon, "lobster tails are just about $19.99 per pound right now, so **how** can you even **try** to justify $36.71 a pound for venison?"

"Okay, look at it this way, Sweetie," I said in a state of domestic terror, "I won't have to spend hardly anything next year! 'Cept maybe for a few broadheads or so! **Besides**, I'm gettin' pretty good at this archery game. Why, you wouldn't believe the group I shot into a tree the other day from my stand while I was (I clear my throat here!) practicing! Why some stranger, a hunter, even made a comment regarding how good my group was!" She just walked away, shaking her head in negative directions and I know I detected a snicker under her breath. Anyway, hurt pride and all, I headed for the sporting goods store.

Wayne, the clerk and owner of the Triple-D greeted me. "Hi, Joe! Can I help you find something?" I saw something suspicious (perhaps humorous?) in his eyes.

"Yes, Wayne. What might you have in the way of a ground blind in camo? You know, something from which I can hunt from the ground next deer season rather than climbing high into a tree? And, while you're at it, is there such a thing as a tool for removing broadheads from trees available?" Wayne laughs at this inquiry.

"Step right over here, Joe. Got this new broadhead extractor in yesterday. Only $89.95 too! But it'll sure save a lot of expense, you know, pay for itself in short order? And that camo blind over there? Just $289.50! But, hey, didn't I just sell you a nice tree stand last summer?"

My face warmed with blood. "Yes."

"What's the problem, Joe, you don't like it?"

"Yes Wayne, I like it alright!" Don't you just hate nosey, rather pushy store clerks?

Then Wayne began laughing as though he'd just remembered some hilarious joke of the recent past!

"Oh! Now I know! Why you're the guy old Jake was telling me about. That was **you** he saw diving butt first out of a tree! Said it was the funniest thing he'd **ever** seen!"

"Did he also tell you of the arrows I shot into an oak tree?"

"Yep. That's precisely why I ordered in this broadhead puller! Figured whoever it was would be lookin' for one."

"Did you by chance happen to tell my wife about my archery equipment expenditures?"

Wayne's face now reddened with a rush of extra blood, "Why, yes. Yes I did. She phoned telling me she was conducting some sort of study on the direct cost comparison of seafood and beef to the **overall** cost of venison. No harm done, I hope?"

"No Wayne, not really. Say, does the video store in the plaza have any Robert Redford tapes for sale?"

I went to the plaza, bought her several video tapes starring Mr. Redford, then brought them home to her. My broadhead puller and ground blind were tucked beneath a tarpaulin in the bed of the truck. As I handed her the Redford tapes, all she said was, "Thanks, Tonto! And even though I do love you, you're still helplessly pathetic! Why, paying $36.71 for venison!"

I walked away and under my breath whispered, "That trip I just made to Triple-D Sporting Goods just drove the price up another $9.99 per pound." It was at that moment I was startled from my meditative state by a hideous clattering coming from Clyde's yard. Apparently, he was making a final lawn cut for the year? And sure enough, as I peeked through the window, I could see his ambitious effort was bound to drive the cost of venison up another few bucks per pound! I could tell by the fragmented arrows flying from his mower discharge hole, hitting his garage and house with tremendous velocity! "Maybe my wife is right," I thought, "Maybe this whole archery hunting idea is pathetic?"

I walked around the neighborhood dejected, feeling alone in the world with my love for archery and the romance of its primordial beginning. The burden seemed even heavier as I saw the "Safety Zone" signs all the neighbors had placed in their yards. I was able to handle this pretty well, but when old Jim Spencer came out to prune his fruit trees in full fluorescent orange attire, I **was** crushed. This was perhaps the proverbial straw that broke this camel's back. I headed home, silently contemplating how much money I'd lose selling off my once-used archery gear.

The yard and general areas around my house and Clyde's seemed uncommonly quiet. The lights were off in our kitchen and I noticed that Clyde had put his mower away without finishing off his lawn. Of course, his mower may have been unable to take any more punishment but, to me, something seemed terribly amiss....

I stepped into the kitchen and switched on the light. I was startled by two archers standing there in full "battle array."

"Welcome back, Tonto!" the two screamed in unison. It was my loving wife and tolerant neighbor, Clyde.

"Clyde and I figured we loved ya enough to join you in this crazy and primitive endeavor of yours! What do you think, Tonto?"

"What do I think?" I said, my eyes tearing in happiness. "What do I think? What do I **honestly** think? One, the price of venison will climb to an all-time high, but so will my mood in the deer woods from this moment on!

29

We'll be the perfect team, predatorily speaking, that is! Thanks a lot, you guys!"

My wife added a note of happy news. "Honey," she said, "I'd like you to know I returned the Redford tapes and with the money I got back, I put a meat grinder and some fine butchering knives on lay-away. I thought that may help cut down on the per-pound cost of venison?"

"You're absolutely right, Sweetheart. And it may also cut down on my time spent in Yonder Woods, huh? Let the new honeymoon begin, Mrs. Tonto!"

Then Clyde broke in with, "Yeah, right! Your second honeymoon will just be starting while my marriage goes to the wolves. My wife picked up those Redford tapes today before they lost the warmth of your wife's hands!"

"Clyde, ol' buddy, there ain't nuttin' like a fall from a high tree stand to take your mind off such trivial civilized matters!" Clyde just smiled but his expression seemed to ask, "You sure of that?"

I shrugged my shoulders and whispered, "Kinda…"

"A War Baby Doubles"


I'm a great believer in the adage, "War babies had it tough in the post-war times." Even though I made it up. I'm speaking, nonetheless, of that vintage of American, born say, between 1942 and '46, one of which I happen to be. Vintage '42, as a matter of record.

Personally, I suffered greatly, albeit indirectly, because of all the activity that went by the name of WWII. I, too, was a victim of sorts, of shotgun "wounds." Not to my tender body, mind you, but to my emotional stability which even today is questionable. Those **were** rugged days, and what we might term "lean." Look, for example, what the war did to Lucky Strike green....

But then, we all had our crosses to bear, so to speak, and many had more than their fair share during those times. It just so happened, I was one of those who had just a little more, almost, than I could bear.

For example, Pap, my father, climbed a warbound ship's gangplank when I was a mere nine-months old and headed for the European Theater. And that, for those too young to remember, wasn't a movie house. Now, being just 9-months old or thereabouts, I couldn't even wave goodbye to Pap, so imagine how frustrating that must have been? And indeed, it must have taken its toll for I recall being told that months afterwards, I would waddle about the house saying, "Bye-Bye Da-Da" all day long—every day! Now when Pap brought home a German souvenir, one item in particular, a German shotgun, 16-bore choked full and full, with barrels as long as broom handles, it was, in essence, my "cross." But, innocent and young, I didn't realize it. . .Not then!

Back then, in the post-war era, homes smelled of fresh-baked biscuits, Half & Half tobacco smoldering in a father's pipe, simmering, beef-laden, homemade vegetable soup, the Old Spice aftershave which most dads wore, a smidgen of dog essence tucked neatly behind the sofa (divan in those times but divans usually had no back or arms, so smarts weren't in great abundance either!) and, come fall, the wonderful aroma of pippins baking beneath a blanket of cinnamon. And last, but certainly not least, the delicious odor of Hoppe's Number 9 filled the entire abode. All of this seemed the perfect blending for any home. . .

It's nice, every so often, to summon those golden memories. It kind of eases the tensions of today's hustle-bustle world of high-tech nestled—not so cozily—in asphalt.

When Pap finally did come home from the war, I recall how he'd busy himself with gun-fondling and cleaning his shotguns and rifles for the seasons upcoming. I was nearing four-years old and Pap gave me my first bottle of Hoppe's and an old Barlow knife with broken blades – looked good to me for a start, I suppose. And I'd just get underfoot, literally, and often follow so closely behind him that if he stopped suddenly, I'd run into his posterior.

I was in this fog of fantasy and I remember clearly how I'd make believe I was going to accompany him to the frosty, amber field across the road from our home outside of Greensburg, PA. That field, now, sadly enough, is a par-3 golf course, thanks to the whims of folks who'd rather beat up a little, white ball than enjoy the best pheasant hunting in the county. That swamp was a sort of sanctuary in those days, and later, I'd be right alongside Pap, knocking down ringnecks. However, for the first few years, I went through this bizarre training period which began when I was 9. During those years, I went along with Pap, my grandfather (Joe Number One), and my uncle on my stepmother's side,

Buck Budd. I carried the traditional weapon for a kid in those days; one I felt was a devastating hunk of weaponry. A Daisy, Red Ryder BB-gun with a strand of rawhide attached to a side-ring for only Red knew what. This gun allowed me to get familiar with the feel of toting a firearm through the fields and woodlots and was the item used for teaching me where—or more precisely, where **not**—to point the muzzle. I also was allowed to swing (though, of course, never shoot) on a game bird now and then, as well as cottontails. Pap would say patronizingly, "You'll learn a little about lead and swing that way, Joey."

One morning while out with the three of them, about one year prior to my **real** hunting debut, Pap said, "Well, next year, Joey, you'll be carrying that German double I liberated from the war." And, had I known then what I was in for, I no doubt would have run away from home. For even though I thought this upcoming affair with the shotgun would be the coming of knowledge and adulthood, it proved far more than that. Actually, I was to be placed on the very threshold of severe emotional stress, a subject which in those days carried little more weight than the Bambi Syndrome; doctors knew precious little about either.

I should point out that my carrying the gang's game for the first few seasons afforded me some clear understanding of the term, "War baby." I thought then, it meant in part, that those of us born during that span in time were destined to fight for—and well earn—any advancement we hoped—or expected—to make. At least that's how it seemed when I was coming up and carrying game that, most times, weighed a great deal more than I.

I **vividly** remember two things that were especially difficult to come by in the fifties, for a kid anyway; these were money, respect, and praise. But that's three things, isn't it? Which I suppose brings up a fourth, straight thinking. What with living under the pressures of forever trying to prove ourselves; and having to live in clouds of pipesmoke and vapors of gun solvents; and painfully having to listen to adult post-hunting chatter from the confines of a basement

33

while cleaning the men's heavy, daily kill – well, we didn't have a whole lot of time for "thinking!" Thinking, then, was often a self-induced mental process for finding excuses to miss school.

I would say praise came hardest, thus we deemed it most precious. For example, had I dropped a charging rhino (there weren't any in Pennsylvania!) with my model 94 Daisy, Pap may have glanced in my direction and just very casually said, "Pretty nice shot, Joey." That, if anything, would have been the full extent of it, never again to be mentioned even in idle small talk among the adults. However, my hurrah was on a fast-approaching wind, and had I known it then, I may have been a bit more unwavering in my ways.

I may have (emphasis on "may!") protested a little about having to clean everyone's shotguns and game after a day of always successful hunting. I may have complained about having to chip (I almost became a geologist because of this. Imagine!) the dried mud from everyone's boots and of having to lug the men's game around all day in the back of my specially-built jacket. It had a **huge** pouch sewn onto it for just that purpose and when full, as usual, the bottom was but an inch or so above ground surface. I always looked as though someone unseen was holding me in a half-nelson! I easily could have been permanently injured from carrying 30-plus pounds of game and extra shotshells all day: "Part of your training, Son. . ." Why, I could even have been blinded by the close, autumn sun for I was forever forced, by the weight, to look straight up and kind of feel my way with shuffling, booted feet through the fields. But I did it and nothing showed up on the X-rays I paid for using my trapping revenues. . .

Still, my most treasured memories in those formative (and nearly crippling!) years as a beginning predator were of Mother's cooking – one-pound cookies which today may easily be compared to Frisbees – and of my first hunt with a real gun. The German, choked full and full. (I later learned,

34

the choke designation was symbolic of the person "fullish" enough to use it in a hunting situation. . .)

One Sunday, just a few weeks prior to my first season, Pap came downstairs with the German double. "Well, Joey, this is the year you'll be hunting with the men, right? Here's the old German side-by-side, wanna fool with it a little?"

I'd of course held it countless times before, however all of my wingshooting training came from Pap's old Ithaca and Grandfather's gorgeous Fox Sterlingworth in 16-bore. I got fair at smoking clays; learning lead, swing-through methods and other things that required instincts more than intellect—thank goodness. But as I stoke the memories, I don't recall Pap mentioning the super bird, the ruffed grouse that forever fascinated me.

I recall there being a good number of them in the grape-tangled hollows near the creeks I angled but all I ever heard Pap say was, "I'll show ya how to shoot grouse when you're a little older, Joey. They're a bit tough for a beginner and frustrate many a veteran too!" And, memory serving accurately, I don't recall ever carrying any for the guys back then. Today, I believe he avoided the ruffed grouse subject because he **knew** the old German double patterned so tightly that it, and the man carrying it, posed no threat to the grouse population....

With the season not far off, the air became filled with the sweetly penetrating smell of Hoppe's #9 and pipesmoke. Enough to move the adrenaline in any hunting man's blood. It was about that time, too, I was permitted the occasional cup of coffee which to my young tongue was strong. Pap always said, "Now that's coffee, Joey! Why, I could probably float a few .300 Savage cartridges in it? Stuff'll keep ya movin' in more ways than one. . ." It was stout and to this day, I make it like Pap did back then.

Our hunting lunches consisted primarily of southern-fried woodchuck from Pap's summertime hunts, which no doubt originated due to matters of economy and modest income. But mothers, special as most are, always had the proverbial ace in the hole, not to mention a little unsolvable mystery about them. Mine carried this very large key pinned to her floral apron with what had to be a Guinness-qualifying safety pin. It was, as we forced her into telling us one afternoon during a moment of rare weakness, the key to what she referred to as "the sweet box." A large, grandfather-made affair housed in our chilly, dark pantry. The lock on which would have been large enough to secure the gates of Fort Knox. Not that she was stingy, but because Pap would go through sweets like a hot Bowie knife through fresh-whipped butter, leaving little more than smell in the box. He attributed this addiction to sweets to the U.S. Army's giving him large rations of chocolate during WWII. And he could—and often would—eat enough peanut butter fudge at one sitting to rot the hull of the Queen Mary oceanliner. Thus, Mother was forced to ration it if we were to have any left for our hunting lunches.

Pap would sometimes retaliate for her securing the fudge as though it were the crown jewels of England. He'd always say things to me so she'd overhear, and she could overhear from the confines of a speeding tank, like, "Why I couldn't shoot a hole through your mother's gravy with my deer rifle!" I'd laugh; she'd wiggle the key in our noses.

Seriously, our lunches would have made a blue-ribbon caterer envious. You'd have thought we were going on safari rather than just a few hundred yards across the road. She was a paragon, however, of generosity with a touch of thriftiness. Meaning woodchuck instead of chicken.

One weekend evening, Pap mentioned he was taking me to town for a new hunting outfit. I protested, to his surprise, because sentimental scoundrel I tend to be, even today, I wanted to wear the old briar-beaten brush pants and jacket he'd recently retired. And I admitted to not wanting to look like a greenhorn to any hunters we might meet afield.

"Those things'll be too sloppy on you," Pap said, "why shoot, the pants're a good foot longer than your legs!"

Mother intervened as usual. "I could alter them a little for him, Frank?"

Nevertheless, I wanted things just as they were, insisting, hopefully, she leave the pants alone and simply pin up the sleeves of the jacket. I used some psychology I'd learned from Pap. "Mom, you have enough to do around here. Heck, I'll just stuff the legs of the pants into my galoshes?" That pretty much settled, I went upstairs to try them on over my Gene Autry pj's.

As I was coming back down the stairs, I picked up the old German double from the gun rack and walked into the den at port arms, at which time Pap broke into a wave of hysterical, hyena-like laughter that would have made Jackie Gleason sound like Cinderella. Even as Mother ran from the room holding her hand over her mouth, I painfully held back my own laughter. Not the least bit easy, but I **knew** if I'd laughed at myself, I'd be forced into a new outfit in my own size. But, even a few minutes later, after I'd gone off to bed, the laughter seemed to be in reserve status or escrow, I had to turn over the pillow to its drier side. . .

The next afternoon, Pap took me out back to have a go with the German side-by. He was hand-flinging them perfectly out into our buffalo grass field and I hit three, smoking them to where little hit the ground. But I'd shot at about fifty! I should have realized then, but in my excitement, I was all but blind and senseless. . .

Grandfather phoned the day before the season to learn of our first-day plans. Pap mentioned we'd be hunting with Buck as usual and reminded Grandfather that this was the year of "Joey with **the** gun." The German, choked full and full, remember. The tubes on it, I'm certain, are some 34-inches long. Adding that to the stock length made me not much taller than the gun when held at what Pap called parade rest.

Buck pulled into the drive the first morning looking like a model out of an L.L. Bean catalog. After the customary greetings and the pouring of the aforementioned, highly authoritative coffee which tasted as wonderfully as all coffee smells, Buck wandered into the den to sit, sip, and compare notes with Pap. When he spied the German double lying open on the sofa, he smiled his million-dollar, but ghoulish smile and asked with a chuckle preceding, "**Who** in the world is going to use that beast?" At twelve, I was considerably naïve, and in this particular case, add to that gullible and vulnerable. . .

Soon thereafter, we left for the swamp across the road. Full of ringnecks, we should have little trouble getting our four, two-bird limits in less than two hours' time.

Pap instructed me, "Load just the right barrel, Joey. It'll teach ya to make the first shot a killing one and get ya used to making certain of the shot before slapping the trigger. . ." What he neglected to tell me, was the old German gun was bored incredibly close; to simply say it shot a tight pattern would have been a gross understatement; thing shot like a rifle up to 75-yards and farther!

I was soon to learn why Buck had snickered when he saw someone was actually going to take the German gun into the field. And lest I forget, there was another thing which was hard to come by in those "good old days." For a kid to get serious conversation out of those making up the world of adults. No one ever said that in order for me to hit game with that thing, especially airborne game, I'd first have to allow it to get into the neighboring county. And, if I expected to mark down what I **did** hit, I'd need good binoculars; possibly an out-of-state license if I planned on retrieving my kill when we hunted near the state line.

By ten that morning, I'd already burned nearly a box of the old, blue Peter's shells Pap gave me (remember the ones with the airborne mallard on the box?) without doing **any** damage to the Pennsylvania game population. I'd missed enough to fill a railroad coal car above the "gunwale," and was beginning to wonder whether the number "6" on the box indicated the year of manufacture as opposed to shot size? My "hurrah" however would be an afternoon event, yet to come. . .

Everyone had their ringnecks except for the kid carrying the shooting broom handles. We talked things over with Buck and Grandfather and the three of them decided we

38

should split up and hit the squirrel woods behind Roadman's lake after a field lunch.

I, of course, went with Pap. He was sleepy as he usually was after hunting in the morning, and it wasn't five minutes after we sat down under an ancient oak that he fell asleep. His last audible words, "Bust a few, Joey. We'll head for home soon." Then off he went sawing a cord per minute, but never losing the pipe he had clenched between his teeth with at least a half-tin of tobacco stuffed into the well-carboned bowl. And to this day, I think it was his unique sounding snoring that brought the squirrels to moving about in the treetops. I know I've tried to emulate the sound numerous times, to no avail. Pap had a nose like no call I've ever seen.

I was apprehensive when I spotted my first squirrel high up in a nearby oak. Hunched up on a branch, perhaps sun-bathing, he had to be all of 70 or 80-feet high. And certainly, by now, I was wondering whether I could hit a barnyard bull at ten-paces with the German double. Unsure, I tapped Pap on the shoulder to ask his advice, while pointing to the stocky gray. "Put the bead just behind his noggin' and squeeze, Joey." Long story real short, I touched off the shot and down came my first piece of Pennsylvania game. Pap apparently heard both the shot and the squirrel hitting the ground, for he gave me a slight "atta-boy" tap on the thigh and fell back into a stentorian sleep. "Praise enough." I thought.

I took three more grays within the next 45-minutes or so. Pap never flinched during the barrage. When I awoke him to leave, he said (without even acknowledging my kills), "Let's work out that grove of pines on the other side of that big section of wild grape tangles. May roust a bird or two outta there if we take 'er slow and easy."

Pap motioned for me to work in a relatively straight line, using his shotgun barrel to point the way and also the directions which I could safely shoot—straight ahead and to my left. As I entered the thickets, I stuffed another hull into the left chamber, somehow feeling certain Pap wouldn't mind. I, too, felt the area might produce a couple of birds and my confidence was high after shooting four squirrels at stratospheric heights—not to mention they were out better than 25-yards from our stand.

As I bent to exit the pine grove, two grouse burse from a covert of wild berry briars, one right after the other! "Bang!" went the first barrel, then "bang!" went the second barrel (choked full and full, remember.) The first of the two birds went down in a puff of feathers while the second continued flying, right wing down a bit, out of sight and into some thick brush but at low altitude. "One outta two ain't bad," I thought.

Just about then Pap bellowed, "What in the blazes was that?"

"Grouse, Pap, two of 'em and I hit one!"

"Well, just keep working straight ahead and I'll meet you at the edge of that next pine grove!"

Worried that I may be in deep doo-dah as they say today, I moved along and in a stand of oak shoots, I saw what a young buck had done to a sapling. As I inspected the rub, I looked around and, in some rather high briars, I spotted the second grouse, deader than a stone! Excited I was, but more so worried about what Pap would do when he realized I'd stuffed in the second round. This brings up yet another intangible difficult to come by back then; getting away with **not** listening to one's parents. Some form of punishment was inevitable. . .

As we approached the creek near our road, Pap took a bursting cottontail. Our hunt was over. We broke open the guns, and headed across the road to the front yard where Buck and Grandpap stood awaiting our field report.

I removed the four squirrels and one grouse from my coat. Grandfather's eyes sparkled and widened as he smiled and said, "Well, Joey, you did real well for a young hunter. Grouse are tough critters to hunt and hit for any man! Grandpap is real proud of you."

Pap interrupted this moment of rare glory. "C'mon now, Joey, show them the rest of what you got today."

"You mean you know?" I asked.

"I'm your father, son. It's my job to know everything about you. 'Specially when you're carrying a shotgun. Come on, now, show them what else you have in that coat."

I could almost feel my eyes wanting to explode! I was under considerable pressure here. I pulled the other grouse from my gigantic pouch and lay it on the ground next to the rest of my game, proud—but at the same time very queasy in the gut. . .

"Now would you look at that, gentlemen!" Pap said, continuing with, "A young man of mine using a shotgun that could easily blow out the bull of a big-bore target at seventy-five yards took doubles on grouse! A gun that if mounted on a Nazi Panzer, may well have won the war for them. Why, a gun so long and awkward that once a man gets to swingin' it, it's nearly impossible to get 'er stopped, let alone hit anything with it. 'Specially if it's moving! Yes sir, that there German job is the real king of swing. Just imagine marking down a bird then getting the second lined up and down while you're swinging like a revolving door! And little Joey here took those four bushytails from so high up in the oaks that they were stiff with rigor mortis before they touched down! Why they were so high, my son there had time to lay down that old German gun, put on a fielder's mitt and catch the critters! And if he's standing there shaking because he thinks I'm about to chew him out for stuffing the second shell in that beast of a shotgun, he's worrying about something that's not about to happen. He's earned the right to carry two shells in the gun and hunt with the men!"

It's pretty tough breaking a sweat in the chill of October when you're just standing around, but I did! As I said, praise was tough to come by back in those days and this behavior from Pap was as rare as finding an emerald in a rooster crop. But, as I recall, Pap was always a generous man. And today he's no different. When he told the story countless times after that day, he always said, "My son, Joey, shot doubles on grouse his first time in the field." That is something that will always be very special to me. One of those quieter gifts many of us derive from hunting.

In those days, precious and priceless as they were, kids were forced by prevailing conditions to mature somewhat early in life, in numerous and various ways. Some by doing a man's work, others by achieving something in the autumn hunting fields which "only a veteran could achieve." In Pap's eyes, I'd become a man through many trials he felt were tough. I had a very long trapline which pretty much supported my wants and needs—which were many. I'd endured the many pains of not carrying a gun in three autumns prior to my 12$^{th}$ birthday and had carried the game and extra shells so the men could hunt comfortably. And after the hunts, took care of **all** the equipment, game dressing and clothing.

As I remember it, Pap, even owning a heating and plumbing business, couldn't easily afford to free me from the pains of using the liberated German gun which shot like a varmint rifle. Times were tough, and the only other smoothbore we had in the family was an old J.C. Higgins with a terrible, terminal case of inverted acne which Grandpap said, "No man deserved!" And later on I would become solitary heir to the masterpiece, Fox Sterlingworth.

So, even though money was indeed difficult to come by in those golden times, I like to think and tend to feel in my heart, that I was quite wealthy in many ways. That is, for just being a war baby in the days of hand-me-down knickers, one-pound cookies, and fathers who taught using love as their main tool as opposed to the ash handle. Fathers who led by example and who displayed their deep, true feelings through twinkling eyes. My wealth was in the form of Buck Budd and a grandfather, Joe Number One, who promised me a gun I'd admired since I could walk. What was more important was seeing that Santa Claus magic in his eyes, that twinkle which could easily shame the twinkling in God's sky. This then, was my true wealth. Then, the reality; today, the memories.

As I write this, my son, Justin happens to be 9-years old. He's already itching to walk the amber fields with his "Pop." Times in our family won't change with regard to life's quality. He wants to carry that old German double his first time out and I may just allow that. Then, once he can take game consistently with that rascal, choked full and full, remember, I have a sweet-swinging old Fox Sterlingworth that will make his hunting days easy. Easy as it will be for him to get into my old, outsized hunting britches, which he already has hanging in his closet. Outside that closet hangs a photo of his grandfather Joe Parry Number One. That which is inside and outside of the closet proves his true wealth.

And this old man hopes fervently to add to it all.


## Epilogue: "A War Baby Doubles"

This piece was written in July 1984. Pap got to read it, Grandfather had been gone 23 years by then. Pap died 10 years after it was first published and the German gun never got to its rightful owner, the boy in this piece. But the Fox today, hangs in my son's bedroom next to his Grandfather Parry's (my Pap) old Savage model 99 in .300 caliber. Justin never got to hunt with his grandfather, never, of course, knew his great-grandfather or Buck Budd. Buck died when Justin was but a sprout.

I speak reverently of the three of them quite often and Justin listens with a magic glisten in his young eyes. And the youth returns to my eyes and heart as I speak. Just one thing that will forever hurt and bother this old man; Justin, as much as I love him and as much as I'd like to change the facts, will never be as wealthy as his father. He knows why, has accepted it but indeed and certainly feels cheated. He's right about that, but as I told him, "Those days are long gone, my Son. But trust in me that I'll forever strive to let you taste the leftovers. . ."

"The Old Timer"

Friends are one of life's greatest gifts, and yes, greatest pleasures, in that relationships often provide us with many priceless times spent together. And, sadly enough, there are those rare times when we meet people whom we immediately know would make a marvelous friend, but for one reason or another we know, too, we may never again see that person; and whether on boat, plane or train, the farewell comes a little hard...

How often have we, as outdoor enthusiasts, found ourselves sharing a log with a stranger while in the field? A stranger who perhaps was very warm and friendly during the short, woodland chat -- one whom you would have liked to know better, but never again saw? I call these short, outdoor-born "friendships" cotton-candy-times, in that they're sweet moments that melt all too quickly.

Since a time further back than I care to recall, I've made a special point to always carry a small notepad and a pencil (ink freezes!) in my jackets during the hunting and fishing seasons. My objective, obvious as it may all ready be, was to never again get caught with my britches at my ankles; I would always be ready for the next amicable stranger and jot down his name should he or she be the type I may want to see again. I'll share here, the why of it all.

To this day, I am sorry about a time I failed to carry pad and pencil, and this comes to you with the hope you'll not make the same mistake. For it may well result in losing something that had the potential of becoming very special and the "what-if" is something that will pull at one's heart for a lifetime.

I was trout fishing a mountain stream-fed pond in the north woods of Pennsylvania. The water was frigid with the spring thaw, and almost too placid and crystalline to fish effectively, but trout anglers are a stubborn breed. The trout, often smarter by far than this angler, seemed overly sensitive and it got to the point where I felt they may be suffering from a lock-jaw epidemic. They were not "taking" anything, save perhaps a nap.

Never concerned much with filling the wicker creel, I settled back and stuffed my pipe with a fistful of Half & Half, and while so doing, watched a white-tailed doe tiptoe to the lake's opposite edge. I let her sip for the longest time, but when she raised her head to inspect the obtrusive sport across the lake's little cove who had his smoking bowl clamped between his teeth, I whistled, as one might to any fair lass, and added a conversational, "Hello little lady!" With that she obviously decided the woods were safer (and saner!) than the lake's edge and scurried toward a stand of pines.

I drank in more of the mountain morning's serenity and summoned a few of yesterday's golden memories, remembering a bit of Grandfather's (Joe Parry, the First) lore. I felt that with one tidbit I'd summoned, I may well be able to entice a trout to my hook, with the hope of dissolving some of the monotony of the morning. And ultimately, I was rewarded with much more—a cotton-candy friendship.

Lazily, I lifted my tired-self from the luxurious bed of spruce needles and begun a lakeside walk to search the shallows for Gramps' secret "stickworms" – more technically, caddis fly larvae. Where these can be found, they're devastating on trout and I soon collected a fistful.

The first, gently-landing cast with "stickworm" in place, produced an immediate take and I had my first trout of the season; small, but in and of itself, a momentous occasion.

Four others of about the same size soon followed suit. And all were released as I was in one of my unindustrious moods.

Out of stickworms, I lay back and lit another pipe, somehow finding the white curl of aromatic smoke mysteriously interesting and soothing. "Reason enough," I thought aloud, "to terminate the stickworm hunting – at least for now."

My idle state was soon interrupted by a soft, gentle voice of broken tongue and European persuasion which came as, "Ah scuzza me, mister."

A moderately robust, older gent in fresh-looking, starched bib coveralls added as I looked up at him, "I no catcha da feesh all da morning. Coulda you pleasa tella me what it isa you usin? You no minda, please?"

I lifted myself from the ground, smacked my pipe bowl into my palm and said, "Why sir, I wouldn't mind at all. Follow me and I'll show you what and how to find them…"

The russet-cheeked old timer did a sort of soft-shoe shuffle to get in step with me and said, "Tanka you mister! A tanka you veddy, veddy much!" He scampered behind me in that lovable, but comical walk of his, very reminiscent of a lab puppy about to be fed. His million-dollar smile cracking his weathered, ruddy cheeks, his eyes twinkling cosmically – eyes and a smile I would not soon forget, if ever.

Within a short time, we'd found enough stickworms to keep him busy for a few hours and, after showing him the larvae worm inside its "house" the old gent exclaimed, "Well I be doggonit, datsa some a ting you show da olda Mario. Tanka you. Tanka you so veddy, veddy much." Assuring him the pleasure was indeed, all mine, I went about showing him how to angle the morsel-like larvae and gave him about a dozen gold-plated egg hooks on which he was to lace his bait. Those he had may have well been tarpon salt water hooks.

After I'd pretty much covered and demonstrated my caddis-larvae fishing method, he removed a small, dog-eared notepad from his bibs and asked, "Woulda you mind veddy much to givva me a you address?" He stood there, smiling, and reminding me greatly of my grandfather who also had that magical twinkling in his eyes. He handed me the notepad in which I was to place my name and address, then thanked me again before leaving for his spot on the mountain pond, shuffling away in that rolly-polly gait.

He must have been at least 75 yards away when I heard his voice ricocheting from the mountainsides, and echoing to where the words all but merged into one. "Tanka you Joe! A tanka you veddy, veddy much!" With that my day was pretty much full of all that I came for, and so, I left.

As I passed above the spot where the old timer sat, I could hear him laughing and assumed my "lessons" were working to his satisfaction. I never thought to get his name and address at the time, but as I drove to the old camp, I felt sure he'd be on the lake the next morning. He wasn't, sadly enough, and I had to head home that following afternoon....

I drove to the lake early and still no Mario. During the months that followed, the precious memory of the old timer never left me for any length of time. The visions of him, his smile, his sparkling eyes of azure blue, were always there; he had made an impression on me and the Santa commercials on TV during the holidays brought him even more vividly to mind, and yes, more often.

Several days after Thanksgiving, the mailman sounded our doorbell and handed me a package. I thanked him, closed the door, and sat to open the bedraggled affair, more wrinkled was the brown paper than a respectable, California prune. On the wrapping, my name and address had been scrawled with a felt-tip pen in what one would graciously refer to as "shaky penmanship." I noticed immediately, that there was no return address on the outside, but still opened it in a manner reminiscent of a toddler demolishing a Santa-delivered Christmas gift, assuming it was from a family member.

Inside was the most beautifully mounted, brown trout of about 15 inches, I'd ever seen. A note lay in the bottom of the box, stating "...it was written by a neighbor, for I cannot

write English well, yet." My eyes jumped to the bottom of
the page, searching, where "Mario" was scrawled, then back
to the beginning to finish the short message. All the while I
read it, my mind and heart translated into how old Mario
might have said it. But this is what was written:

> Dear Joe:
> I hope you and your family have a
> wonderful Christmas. I thought you
> would like to have this fish I caught on a
> stickworm at the lake that day I met you.
> It was my very first in America and the
> biggest I caught that day.
>
> I will look for you this spring if you are
> coming to the lake but if I do not see you
> there, Joe, thanks again for sharing your
> stickworm secret with me. Every time, I
> catch a fish or see a stickworm, I will
> think of you, my friend. I will always
> remember you.
>
> Thank You.
> God bless you,
>
> Mario
> Merry Christmas)

A small, brass plate beneath the colorful, mounted
trout read: "For my friend Joe—Mario's First American
Fish"

Through rather puddle, glistening eyes, I soaked in
the beauty of the mounted trout and smiled, as I vividly
visualized the old man. How very special he was....

I returned to the mountain lake that next spring, but
heaven must have written a script I didn't fully understand.
Seeing the old timer again, apparently was not to be. And no,
I never saw him again and no one in the area of the lake, nor
the small village nearby, knew of him. I almost brought
myself to believe the old European from across the Big Pond
was merely a marvelous dream, but indeed, I knew he was
for real. I wanted so badly to thank him, to once again feel
the vise-like, warm grip of his sincere handshake, but no....

As I write this, I can clearly see the mounted trout, the framed letter with his scrawled, shaky signature. I often sit and savor his memory and the greatly-missed, cotton-candy time, his million-dollar smile. Wherever he is, I pray he knows how grateful I am for the priceless lesson he taught me, that being, to always carry a notepad, and to forever retain my sharing ways....

And somehow, even today as I angle in the mountains of northern Pennsylvania, I wishfully anticipate someone tapping my shoulder and saying in a soft, gentle voice of broken tongue, "Ah scuzza me, mister..."

[AUTHOR'S NOTE: Few things in life provide more joy than a daughter and I've yet to discover a single "thing", save a son, which is an equal in this regard.

This story, like the others in the book, is true and became nationally known, recognized as one of the few stories penned in modern America that changed the wrongful thinking of the non- or anti-hunters nationwide. It seems from some of the letters I received praising this piece (I never thought it would sell!) that those who do not hunt, or even remotely understand the hunters of America, felt we were heartless, calloused and uncaring, bloodthirsty "beasts." Not so. Not even close ....

As for the young lady in "To Cry for Waxwings," the reader will have to decide whether she ultimately went to the autumn woods with Pop, rifle in hand. I can only tell you this: I fully understood her sentiments; after all, she is blood of my blood, though perhaps, a touch softer in the heart?]

## "To Cry for Waxwings"

Imagine, if you will, a little girl with long, flowing, silken hair that could put the beauty of a full autumn moon to certain shame. Her smile warm enough to melt the calloused heart of a barbarous dictator. And a laugh so terribly contagious and tender you feel there should be some exotic law prohibiting it, but deep down you're glad there isn't.

This little girl with a walk so cute, so wonderfully unique, delicately feminine, you feel a hug from your manly father's arms might hurt her. And so, you often wait until your emotion and love is a little more in control before you do. To yourself, you describe her walk as that of a happy little penguin.

And again, imagine a kiss "good night" so warm and wondrous it leaves your heart begging and aching for just one more – long after she's gone to bed. Could this describe your little girl? I know I was blessed with one just like this, and I'm having a terrible time deciding just how I'm going to place a high-powered rifle into her soft little hands, train her to shoot it, then in my deep baritone voice, say "There ya go! Now go kill a deer, sweetheart!"

Little lady that God made her, she nevertheless loves the taste of venison and the fact that Pop shot it matters not. She was literally raised on it and again, little lady that she is, she has predatory blood chemicals coursing within her system. However deep they may be, they still exist. Like the folks in the Ragu commercials used to say, "It's in there!"

A few years back an urgent writing assignment consumed my most favored deer season. I'd not missed one in nearly forty years and it hurt. Then, and now, that hurt lingers, still today. It meant a winter without venison and my children and I cherish these meals of wild bounty with unique reverence. This would be the first and hopefully the last winter we would suffer through without the sacred deer meat ….

The aforementioned little girl's birthday falls in May and days before the 10th of that month, I asked her what she'd like Poppa to get her for her birthday. "Do you want to know what I'd really like, Pop?"

"Yes, honey, what?"

"I'd like to have venison steaks for my birthday supper!"

Immediately, I began to entertain thoughts about poaching, but it never went beyond that, for people who know me often refer to me as "The Preacher." I've always had a personal vendetta against poor field ethics and the illegal (or careless!) taking of game. So honestly, the poaching thought never got to any level of serious deliberation.

So what does a father do, in May of the year, to place venison on his daughter's birthday dinner plate? They don't sell the stuff! I did, though it shames me to admit it, consider begging a local game commission officer for a warm, not too damaged roadkill. After all, a man has a cuddly, loving daughter for far too short a time, and during those precious, priceless years he ought to bust his ever-loving derriere to fill her every want and need ....

This lack of venison made me distraught and feeling as helpless as I'd ever felt. It's my job, the job of all "Pops" everywhere, to fill dreams and wishes, and personally, it always filled my heart when I was able to accomplish what were sometimes small miracles. It brought my deep love of fatherhood to its emotional apex.

Then one afternoon, just prior to her birthday, I mentioned my dilemma to a neighbor, not knowing he had a cache of venison in his freezer. Bless his hunting heart, he walked to his deep-freeze, plucked out two packages of backstraps and handed them to me. "Here," he said, "tell Erika to have a happy birthday!"

In a sense, I was saved this time, by the 30-06 my neighbor owned. And I felt justified accepting the venison, for I'd spent considerable time sighting-in the cantankerous old mauser he killed the deer with. We had it grouping nickel-sized clusters consistently at 100-yards. I recalled his words that afternoon at the range: "This old beast never shot so well, Joe! I owe ya one ...." His debt, now, of course, is off the books. (Never was one to hold a debt between friends and/or neighbors!)

I convey all of this because I felt that if she so loves the taste of venison, then she must learn to provide it for herself. Soon, and for all those times after Poppa leaves this fine Earth. Thus, she must learn to hunt, right? And soon she would come of hunting age, so I approached (tentatively!) her mother regarding The Matter ....

"I'm not allowing you to take our little girl deer hunting!" That pretty much settled things? Well, perhaps in the beginning "arguments". However, before studying

52

biology, I cracked a few law books and at one point, felt F. Lee Bailey may have to sit in my backseat, so ….

After relentless cross-examination, Mother came up with, "How is she going to shoot one of those big guns, anyway?"

My reply: "Rifles, dear. As in this is my rifle, this is my gun. You see, a pistol is a gun. Remember the story I told you about my Army drill instructor?"

Nearly squealing, she answered, "Regardless! She's a lady and she shouldn't be out deer hunting with her father!"

I defended, "Honey, is that not better than her getting involved with some brain-dead, pimply meathead boy in her school? At least she'll be safe with me in the deer woods!"

My wife looked over at Erika, arms crossed over her heaving chest, and Erika smiled, exposing those celestial dimples, deep enough to mix cake batter in.

She shrugged her shoulders, tilted her angelic head to where her silken hair fell to one side like a wonderland waterfall and said, "I do love venison, Mom!"

Mom studied her daughter but a few seconds, then said, "Well, if you're going to hunt with that nut you call your father, you can use one of his guns! We don't need another gun in this house! I can't vacuum or dust around the guns as it is!"

I cut in to terminate this "gun" madness. "In three sentences, dear, you used the term 'guns'. They're *rifles*, sweetheart, rifles!"

She had me bewildered regarding my being prohibited from buying just one more gun – pardon, *rifle*. Certainly I was pleased with her decision to allow Erika the privilege and option of hunting with me, but as far as "… not needing another 'gun' in the house!" That hurt. Since we have but three-dozen between my son Justin and me! And yes, it is true, as written so many times, a man never has quite enough 'guns.' However, I was pussyfooting through a minefield here and felt I'd best tread lightly….

"Okay, Erika, how do you feel about all of this? Would you like to attend hunters' education classes this fall and hunt deer with Justin and Poppa?"

"I don't know, Poppa. I'm still not sure I could kill a deer."

"Honey, listen. That's something your heart will dictate when the moment presents itself. For even though everyone, deep down inside, has a hunter in them, not all of us are cut out, as they say, to kill when the time comes. Your Grandfather Parry hunted some eighteen years and never once shot a deer! And, hey, that's okay! What with all the hunters out there today, things are perhaps a little out of biological balance, in that there is far less huntable land. Erika, God and Nature are pretty much one and the same, and it seems as though things are pretty much taken care of out there when needed. Always on a pretty even keel, so to speak. If you decide you don't want to shoot when the time comes, don't pull the trigger! You'll know in your heart, 'Rik, what's right for you and what isn't. Just take hunters' ed and we'll go from there, okay?"

"We'll see, Pop, but for now, how 'bout answering this question?"

"Shoot, sweetheart!" I thought this was going to be another question about rifles or deer hunting...."

"Pop, do you remember that little waxwing bird we found hurt and sick?"

"I sure do; why?"

"Okay, now. You love hunting deer more than anything in the world, right?"

"Well, not quite. I love just being with you a whole lot more!"

"Pop! You know what I mean! You're an outdoor writer and, in a way, you hunt for a living. You're supposed to be rough and tough, right?"

"Kinda..." I answered, wondering feverishly where she was going with all this questioning.

54

"Well, then, tell me. How come you can kill a deer and yet the day that little cedar waxwing died after you'd tried so hard to nurse her back to normal, you cried?"

"I never cried when that bird died!"

"Poppa. I saw the tears on your cheeks when you were burying her out back!" I was had, as they say....

"Okay, honey, let me try to explain. You see, most hunters have more love for wildlife, because of their understanding of it, than the people who don't hunt, at least in some ways. I suppose it's because we're so much more aware of the hardships wildlife species face, day in and day out. We're out there much of the time between early autumn and, say, late January, when the weather is the worst and the snows are the deepest. We're able, then, to see, and it is hurtful, what the animals are up against most of the time, just finding enough food to make it through the winters. Their struggles are, at best, exhausting, which is why I've always held to the old adage that the bullet is more merciful than time. That's why most hunters love animals so deeply, domestic or wild. Animals of the wild are very special to most of us, though, and we're pretty much able to relate to most of their hardships."

"Is that why you cried when the waxwing died, Pop?"

"Honey, a hunter's heart is almost always an understanding heart. Especially when it comes to an animal dying. When I placed that little waxwing into the ground, I felt it died without purpose. Without sound reason, biological or otherwise. But then, I'm not God, and cannot try to play God. But, still, I don't understand death without purpose and, even though I always question it, I probably shouldn't."

"As I patted down the dirt on the little bird's grave, Erika, I could almost see its entire, short life passing before my mind's eye. I could see it in its little speckled eggshell. A mere embryo in what must have been a warm, strange darkness. I thought perhaps it wondered just what it was doing in there, unable to move about freely. What that wall

55

was around her, or whether it even thought about anything? Who knows, honey, how animals and little birds think, or if they think before they're born? Anyway, I could envision that little unfeathered mass growing stronger and bigger. Finally, outgrowing the size of its confining capsule, and I could well-picture the little bird struggling in an attempt to escape the shell. Its matchstick legs kicking, hell-bent for freedom, for daylight. Squirming in a courageous effort to have a look-see at the world outside, a world it knew nothing about, no knowledge of what lay in store for it once it saw daylight, yet still it wanted to know!"

"Then, I could picture the fuzzy little poult patiently awaiting food delivery from its parents, little mouth opening with every movement of the limb on which the nest rested. Just waiting and hungry for a simple grub worm or bug, and totally dependent on the parent birds."

"Feathered now, the little waxwing was able to move about the nest. I could envision it struggling some more, in an effort to mimic the mother's flight. The constant falling and the continued efforts to get it right, so Mother would be proud. Up, down. Up and down, then finally, and beautifully, up, and soaring high above the woodland floor! The hard-found accomplishment of sustained flight came, but after considerable pain and relentless efforts. And its reward for all this? Only that it could now fend for itself. Yet another struggle – a constant, in the life of all wild things.

"And that little waxwing beauty had to die in its first few months of life? Erika, it all seemed very unfair to me. Very final, hurtful, and without purpose, and I didn't have the answer to 'why?' Now, what does my telling you all of this have to do with your deer hunting?"

"Nothing, Poppa. I just wondered how someone as soft-hearted as you can hunt and kill deer, that's all!"

"Honey, I suppose I hunt because I am soft-hearted. I suppose, too, it's my strange way of coming to some understanding of life and, yes, of death. Perhaps it helps me to better understand how very precious life is, when I try to take the life of an animal. I try not to defend or to justify my love of the hunt, or the final act I perform out there in the woods. Hey, God made *me* what I am and if He didn't want me to hunt and kill animals, then He would make the taste of killing a little more bitter for me than it is. I don't always question why I hunt, or why I kill game animals. But, Erika, if I didn't feel hunting was the best method for keeping wildlife in the proper balance, which is indeed for their own benefit, or if I didn't hurt after each and every kill – which I always do – I would certainly question myself more.

"In a way, Erika, deer are like beautiful flowers. When the flower-garden gets too thick, regardless of the delicate beauty of each individual flower, they must be thinned in order for the garden to flourish. And the others will one day have to be thinned, which means dying. I guess, honey, that death is the only feasible way to make way, or room, for new life? And a hunter knows this more intimately than those who choose not to hunt."

"Poppa! You have tears in your eyes, again!"

"Those aren't tears, Erika. Now go over there to the rack and pick out a rifle. Try that little one, with the blonde stock. It's a 7mm-08 and old Pop thinned a few flowers with that one!"

"Okay, Poppa, I'll try out the rifle, but I may never hunt or kill a deer!"

"I know, honey, I know…"

"I love you very, very much, Pop."

And I love you, Erika. More than you'll ever realize….

AUTHOR'S NOTE: This is the story of a young man who captured my heart in 1975, the year of his birth. And he hasn't let go of it yet, as the story tells. . .He's symbolic of what we all should be out there in the hunting wood. I, of course, taught him the fundamentals of shooting, hunting and respect for wild things and places. But this young man, alone, refined it all to form a sort of religion. His ever-deepening respect for wildlife, to this day, brings my eyes to the watering point and my heart to just beyond overflowing. As I write this annotation, May 8, 1997, I think I may safely say his hunting days for those species we most loved to hunt together as he was coming "up" are pretty much over. Oh, I imagine there will be the odd grouse, perhaps even a wild turkey, but little else. Something inside of me switched off not long ago, and about the same time, Justin's enthusiasm to kill as a hunter burned out to where it barely smolders. Perhaps a little autumn breeze will bring it to the flaming point once again? Only one man knows. The fine one in this story and his true Maker. Of course he's my son, Justin…

## "Broken Silence"

Hunting and time spent in the woods are as natural to him as trips to the Little Boy's Room—and very nearly as necessary. But this day, not so long ago in autumn, had to be different even though he and his son had shared the first grouse hunt of the year several times before. It was time for him to let go of the young man he still felt, in heart and mind, was "his little boy."

He must be allowed to discover the magic of hunting alone. The father thought, "Let him feel the quiet, taste the pungent, almost tangible woodland air created by the decaying forest litter." The hollow below their home would allow the young man a certain peace, a needed peace. And a feeling of confidence that every man needs before he can consider himself a man. And so, with a feeling of pain greater than a root canal, he said to his son, "Naw. You go on ahead by yourself. I don't feel much like hunting today." Certainly it was a white lie, but the kind which a mutual God, at times like this, excuses?

He watched as "his" young man laced his boots and dried the FP-10 oil from his Red Label over/under with the same excitement inside him as he felt when readying himself for the first grouse hunt—any hunt. Only this time he felt a sort of emptiness that didn't blend well with the excitement. It would be his son's first time out alone; the cord was severed. . .

He questioned his son about how to handle things out there, navigate hills safely, be careful of hidden acorns beneath the leaves, when to shoot and when to hold back? And there was the last minute briefing on lead and pointing, not aiming and yes, they came from an apprehensive, empty heart. And he knew all the while the instruction wasn't necessary. For the young hunter knew these things, and well.

The Old Man wanted so badly to go, but no, not this time. This was a sort of gift to his son. Not truly his to give, but indeed his to share. The young man attended to things quietly and his face revealed the need he'd had for quite some time. The need to go it alone, if just this once, this first time. "We all need our space, our private moments. . ."

"See ya later, Pop! Don't worry, I'll be just fine. . ." And sure he'd be fine. He was fine when he began hunting years ago. He was well-schooled in all aspects of the hunt; the safety, the overall appreciation of wild places and wild things, be they tree, plant or animal or bird. At age twelve, he seemed a veteran, but then he endured the pains of having an outdoor writer for a father to include getting his tender, two-year old shoulder bruised by a 16-guage side-by-side good old Pop held to it, telling him, "Pull the trigger, Justin." Never before or since were his eyes opened wider. And often, old Pop laughed to himself when he summoned the memories of the long-ago time.

The field before the house slopes away gradually at first, then drops abruptly into a marshy area. Pop could see "his" hunter's Ten-Mile orange glowing in the morning sun, perhaps 150-yards away when he remembered the chokes. He hollered, "What chokes do you have in?" The answer stating modified and improved arrived clearly to his near-deaf ears. "I should have known he'd know that much. . ." But there is always the slightest strand of cord, never visible, but still, attached. "He'll be just fine. . ."

He watched until his son knifed his way through the whippy scrub oak, certain, he thought, to teach him a lesson in handling a little pain without having someone there to complain to that—seemingly—eases the severity and discomfort of it all? And soon thereafter, his hunting companion was out of sight, out of reach but, no, never out of mind or heart. The Old Man would live out this morning's hunt, moment by moment, in his mind's eye. For as always, he walked with his son in spirit. . .

Soon the young hunter would be negotiating the old, rusted barb-wire fence, one they always joked about. "Doesn't look as though this fence line ever held anything in or out!" Then his son would be following Orphan Creek for a ways. A brook which to their knowledge, no one ever bothered naming, and so they did. Thus it was "their" brook, their woodland friend, however dry in autumn it was still a special place to them. "Just a little creek, that's all!" That's what the county natives said of it. Just a little creek, yes, but too, the path to a marvelous grouse covert that seemed to forever defy the cycle of the grouse populations and always produce at least a few birds, year after year. "I hope he brought number eight's," thought the Old Man. Knowing, deep down, he had of course. For in so many ways, his young hunter was a veteran at the age of 12.

Down through the hemlocks, past Time-Forgotten Orchard his son would go. All the while ready, but never fully, for the thunder of a grouse flush. "He shouldn't be too tensed-up through the hemlocks. . .knows there aren't any birds in there til the snow flies." But then, after the grove he would again come to Orphan Creek, follow it a while then come into a whole different cover type—some of which a field mouse would scorn as far as being uncomfortable navigating. Berry thickets, multi-flora rose tangles and a general potpourri of seemingly impenetrable vegetation that seemed never to succumb to cooler or even cold weather. It was always there, always thick and tough going but yes, always held more than a day's bag of ruffed grouse. He and his son didn't refer to this magical place as a covert, but instead, a cradle. A place wherein Mother Nature seemed to forever hide Her favorite birds—each and every year. The Old Man always said, "Blows big holes in the biologists' cycle theory, doesn't it. . .?"

The Old Man thought to himself, "I'll just stand out here on the deck and listen for his shots." And all the while, small prayers came from his lips. "Please, if there's a Red Hunting God looking down right now; give my young man a break. He's not yet tasted the thrill of downing a grouse. Just this one time, for I surely don't want him spoiled into thinking it's an easy game. But give him two, if you would, barely angling birds rather close and don't let them startle him so much that he doesn't even get off his shots. He's an awfully fine young man you know?"

And Pop thought he could almost hear his son's careful but anxious boots whispering their way through the fallen leaves. He could envision his son's widening eyes in anticipation of what surely lay ahead. And he recalled what his son once said about the hemlock boughs as they passed through there one day. A branch tip had brushed his son's chilled cheek and he smiled while recalling his son's words: "Geez, Pop, even though I never had one, that felt as soft as a young girl's kiss! I never realized how soft those needles were. . ." And at the time, Pop laughed and said he himself often wondered what was nicer. A kiss from the bough of a hemlock or a fair-haired lassie; that it was a toss-up to his way of thinking. . .

About now, his son should be into the grape tangles just before the thicket. About 20 or so yards from their beloved Cradle. "No shots yet? Must be he's not quite into it?" Nearly an hour passed and all was quiet in the hollow; no sounds at all some three cups of coffee later. "He's fine. Just poking along as he always does?"

He'd taught his son well; that they hunted not primarily to kill, even though it was a part of the intention. They hunted also to seek challenge, learn of peace and wild things and the platter of grouse drenched well in wine sauce with a hearty side of parsleyed potatoes was simply a bonus for their efforts. "You always come home with something, Son, even if it's not in your game pouch."

He imagined he could hear his son's heart pounding and, if he closed his eyes, he could "see" his knees trembling, readying himself for what no man is ever totally ready for—the thunder of a grouse flush. But was it to be that day?

Some three hours later he could see from the window that "his" hunter was headed home. But even from the almost 300-yard distance Pop thought he could see the young hunter smiling? The binoculars proved him right. "Ahh yes! Thank you God! You have given him something he'll never forget, his first grouse. Perhaps a brace?"

"Grouse," his old man would always preach to him, "are forever better than the men who hunt them when it comes to being alert, ready and furtive, even using trees to their fullest advantage when flying away." Surely this day's success would cultivate a confidence level in him that would breed forever; something he needed. Something all young hunters need in conjunction with sound common sense in every hunting venture. And this hunter of his, Justin, had the good sense and the maturity of a seasoned hunter from Day One but lacked, somewhat, that all- important confidence level that allows a hunter to know well his limitations and to use them to his advantage and in all fairness to himself and his quarry. Pop would always torment him good naturedly, that when it came to grouse it didn't matter what the legal limit was. "Heck, Justin, you never shoot when they flush!" But all the while, Pop knew Justin's day in the sun would arrive and he would be truly deserving of that time.

He once said to his father, "You know what, Pop? I'm kinda glad grouse are like they are. You know, flushing like thunder, breaking the silence and catching hunters off guard. Even though I want one so badly I can feel it all year long, it's something I'm strangely grateful for. I guess it gives me the secure feeling that grouse will always be out there for hunters and that if they ever do disappear, it won't be because of overhunting. You know?" And sure, Pop knew. It was his job to know these things. About grouse, about his son.

Pop hollered from the deck. "How'd ya do, Partner?" Justin then about 100-yards from the house. He just shrugged his shoulders and smiled, not answering with anything. "He got one, by golly!" Pop was thinking aloud, almost tap-dancing on the deck. "He's just being coy with his Old Man!" But, as the hunter got closer to the house, Pop noticed there wasn't anything tethered to his belt. "He knows to keep birds cool and not put them into the heat of his game pouch!"

"Where are they, Partner? Got into them did you?" The young man had this look of peace in his eyes and on his face. A look that Pop wouldn't soon, if ever, forget. To this moment in time, he hasn't, either. For that "gift" given to him by his father, that certain freedom of hunting alone in a seemingly enchanted hollow, would last his son a lifetime; last until he, too, gave his own son that precious, priceless "gift" of freedom, responsibility, trust and yes, the faith that his children would do all that which is right during these sacred autumn rituals. And take special care of that which has been entrusted to all mankind by the Maker Of It All. . .

"They were there, Pop! Just like you said and we both thought they'd be, but, no, I never even warmed my gun barrels. It was the most magical thing I've ever seen! All was so unbelievably quiet in the hollow this morning, you know, like you always said, I could almost hear the dewdrops evaporating. I even walked up on a bedded doe and she didn't seem afraid. Like it was a day of peace among everything living, she wasn't the least bit spooky and just lay there as though I belonged, as though I wasn't a threat. I even whispered a good mornin' to her and got so close I could see the texture of her wet, black nose. Weird morning.

"That doe wasn't but forty or so yards from the Cradle so I was taking it slow and quiet. I was ready. Had it well set in my mind that I wouldn't come unglued at a flush. And I no sooner got into the edge of the Cradle when that strong, sort of muffled sound of wingbeats sounded to my left. I watched it carve its way through the trees as fast and confident as God would allow. Then another one flushed seconds later and I watched it, too. Then another, another and another and yep, another! Six all together and I followed each one of 'em smooth and easy. Pop, it was beautiful! Like a dream come true and more exciting than anything I've ever seen before in any season! Six grouse from our very own Cradle!"

Pop, bewildered and in awe with the relating of Justin's story which seemed contradictory to his longtime dream of killing a grouse or two asked, after clearing his choking throat but still sounding soprano-like, "And you never shot at one? How many could you have grassed?"

"Of the six, Pop, probably four if it were legal but two were real easy shots and I know they could have been mine! I was just so taken back with the magic of it all! I could even see the bands of their tails, the unbroken male bands and the broken bands of the females! That's how close they flushed. It was beautiful. So much so, at first I forgot to shoot then decided after the first three flushed that I wouldn't regardless of how many burst out of there. It was so quiet, Pop. Even though they sure broke the silence of a beautifully quiet morning, it somehow seemed fitting, just right. You know, natural like? In the moment it all took to unfold, I made my decision right then to just drink it all in and let 'em fly on until another day. That was a magic moment for me and one I'll never forget and you know what, Pop? It most likely wouldn't have been the same had you been there with me. Too, it was almost as though you had it all planned for me, 'course I know better. Geez, how many times in all of your hunting years have you seen a half-dozen grouse flush from the same cover?

"I remembered that verse you made me read a while back by the Prophet, Gibran, where he said something about beauty not being a need but an ecstasy? And that beauty isn't a mouth thirsting nor an empty hand stretched forth but, instead, a heart enflamed and a soul enchanted? I remembered that verse real well and I'll tell ya, Pop. My doggone heart was on fire this morning and the rest of me was full enough that killing those grouse didn't seem all that important right then. A morning of wonder, this one Pop!"

What does a father say at times like there? Very little, if anything. His son had found and learned that which he was sent forth to find and learn. Though certainly, this will never cease to amaze fathers as long as there are moments like these. Moments that come from understanding that sons and daughters mature on their own and yes, quickly and easily. And by just simply "pointing" them in the right direction, giving them some space, freedom and love. . .

The Old Man couldn't help but recall the sentiments of Aldo Leopold in his famous "Sand County Almanac," discussing the odd virtue one finds in hunters, since often they only need answer to their own conscience, having no human audience to judge their actions. A father, in this case, may add to that; in that at this moment of truth experienced by the young hunter whereby he was offered his dream-come-true, only he can decide what to do with the moment, the opportunity. It is a personal choice; and this young man, by his own choosing, decided to let the mystery and beauty of this morning marinate, magically, in his heart. . .

"Well, Son, come on into the house. The soup is hot and we'll sit and talk about your morning." That look of peace and a heart-born smile continued to adorn the young man's face.

"Justin you've been wanting to kill a grouse since I bought you that Red Label years ago! Hard to believe you chose to let 'em fly off like that. But, hey, I respect your choice and, in my own way, understand why you let 'em fly. And heck, you needn't worry none; the old red hunting gods'll pay you back one day soon."

"I hope you're right, Pop, cause I'd like to, if you don't mind too much, go out alone again in the morning? Just to see if they're still in the Old Cradle and whether I can walk up again like I did this morning?"

"No problem, Partner. My old back is killing me anyway, so you go on ahead, enjoy yourself. I just hope you're as lucky tomorrow as you were today. I could sure handle a grouse or two for dinner this week, so give some thought to shooting a bird or two."

The next morning, the Old Man heard his young hunter tiptoe across the deck. He got out of bed to watch his son finally disappear into the hollow, this time, wishing more than ever, he were with him. The strand remains forever connected, no matter the time. . .

Some time later, the Old Man saw the young hunter coming through the field with that ever-present bounce in his young legs. He strained to see whether there were birds tethered to the belt of his son. Using the binoculars, revealed nothing but a smiling red face; no birds could be seen.

"He's being cute again! Probably had 'em hidden in his game pouch?" But there were no sounds of gunshots earlier and the Old Man always seemed able to hear such things—usually.

"Well, Partner, how'd ya do this time? Find those birds again or not?" The young man was but a few steps from the deck, checked his Red Label and set it in the crook of where the house joins the porch then sat down on the step.

Smiling and looking up into the Old Man's eyes, he said, "Couldn't keep the Red Label quiet this morning, Pop! I think I could have shot right alongside you and Osgood today!" With that he lay two, plump grouse at his father's slippered feet.

Pop exploded! "All right! Congratulations Partner! Two birds first time shooting is great! How many did you flush?"

"Only five this time, Pop. Rascals held tight with the misty rain and all. I figure the sixth bird just sat in there with all the action going on. These two just exploded from the Old Cradle, about thirty-feet in front of my gun but they did give me a little angle. One went left and the other kinda veered toward the first one just after I shot. After those two went down, three more went outta there. So with that sixth bird and those three, that ought to be enough for the seed you always talk about, huh Pop?"

"Wait a second. How many shots did you fire?"

"Just the two, Pop, why?"

"You mean you got doubles on grouse first time shooting? That's crazy! I sure expected the old red gods to pay ya back for your shining ethics and deep-felt appreciation for the wild Old Cradle and its magic, but doubles on grouse first time around? Sometimes those old gods are just too doggone gracious!"

"You're probably right, Pop, but do you know what? It's my turn to pay them back for their generosity."

"How do you propose to do that, Partner? You have a whole season ahead of you and it'll take a ton of restraint from now on, now that you got a good taste of wingshooting?"

"Well, Pop, I figured I'd let you hunt the Old Cradle from here on out. You know you usually miss the first few grouse of the season and, in a sense, my letting you have dibs on the Cradle is the same as giving something back, or better yet, just not taking anymore grouse from the Cradle this year!"

The father and son laughed at that and went on into the house where two bowls of yesterday's soup awaited them on the dining room table. The same table where two grouse, drenched in wine sauce would be steaming on the morrow— more than the Old Man was steaming today but, with a father's pride. For from the death of two grouse came the

67

birth of a fine hunter who belongs, of course, to himself. . .even though the strand of cord will forever be a strong connection between father and son as it always has.

## "The Royal Roachman"

Barnum and Bailey would undoubtedly relinquish every penny of their cotton candy or corn-dog revenues to buy the rights to exhibit a man who has fingers just about the size of overstuffed summer sausages. And they'd pay more just to watch him wrap a fly at the vise...

Such, however, are the appendages of one Big Bill, the larger member of the Bullseye Bunch, Infallible. An organization consisting of just two men, worlds apart in some respects, but they almost lovingly tolerate one another's aggravating antics. And indeed, they share considerable time together hunting or fishing or anything else even remotely tied to either pursuit.

Joe, leader and much smaller member of this fun-loving, two-man rank & file, constantly felt the need to steer Big Bill in a direction that may ultimately deem him a more respected, prolific "sportsman." But good old, softhearted Joe may have carried this too far when, one evening, he decided to instruct Big Bill in the art of fly construction. Be that as it may, Little Joe loved Big Bill; they were best of friends, and so, Joe greatly enjoyed sharing his vast knowledge, which was rather restricted to the outdoor "sport." Joe preferred to call hunting and fishing, "challenges."

Joe felt, after diving headlong into the task of teaching Big Bill fly tying, he might have been better off teaching Dick Butkus to crochet? Nonetheless, let the all-thumbs lessons begin…

"Billy me boy, you shall be introduced this evening to the fine and delicate art and science of intricate fly construction which, your leader feels certain, will tug at your rapt heart for countless years to come."

"Why," asked Bill, "construct the pesky little things when I can catch all I need on that super-sticky paper a feller can buy?"

Joe quickly learned at that moment, just what he might be in for this time! "Billy, ol' pal-o-mine, I do not refer here, to the common, maggot-bearing house fly, so please open wide the gates of your childish mind and listen intently to the Master of Puritan fly-fishing ways. You will soon thereafter have learned an art and science that will become a pleasant, yet often frustrating, addiction which has its just rewards. You will learn to create your own feathered versions of the things trout most love to molest or disdain and, although often the latter, when the former is done to near perfection the joy is boundless, overwhelmingly, satisfying in fact!"

"You will first become somewhat of an amateur entomologist, then I shall teach you to be an expert tier of flies. And ultimately, my chubby friend with fingers like kielbasa, you will become a respected fly fisherman among your peers. Trust my judgment, Willy, when I say you, my fat, worm-slinging friend, will adore, wholly, the whole package. And indeed, you will adore more your beloved leader for introducing you to the vise and materials of the fly tier. I've little doubt, if in fact we are able to entice your banana-like fingers to function in such an intricate, delicate way. Now, if you would, please sit there, Billy, and shut up as I engage my talents at the vise and please, don't interrupt me, but do learn, if you can."

"What's that enema-ology, Short Stuff?"

"Not enema-ology, Bill! Entomology! It's the study of insects, actually. You first learn some of the insects trout favor most, match them by tying flies that closely resemble them in size, shape and color and, bingo! Take the flies to yonder stream and fish them for the ever-elusive trout. I believe behavior of the fly is most important of all, Billy, then size, shape and color, but I try hard to get it all just right. There's a lot of trial and error, but the rewards of tossing a fly line adorned with your own creation is wonderfully satisfying. It's, to my mind, the only way to angle, big buddy!"

Big Bill smiles broadly, saying, "I have a head start, Joe! Why I studied insects all the time when I was a kid. Shoot, I musta squashed a trillion of 'em in my hands. Then I'd just sit there for hours hours an' hours starin' at their tweeny-weeny guts! Shoot, there was some days I'd go home lookin' like a surgeon who'd just performed a triple bypass! Hands bloodier than a butcher's! I know bugs, little buddy, b'lieve you me! Why, I studied bug guts til I finally graduated school, you know, the fifth grade? Heck, I had years of learnin' 'bout enema-ology, Joe. It's what I did in class to pass time."

"Ento, Bill! Not enema, please! Okay, big guy, you know bugs, now please sit there now and be quiet while your furtive, artistic leader shows you how to tie one that's sure to catch trout come spring."

"What's furtive, Joe?"

"Never mind, Bill, just watch!"

Joe wrapped a fair-looking Adams on a size 14 hook, speaking to Bill as he tied. "Billy, this here fly is what a fellow might use to do what they call, search the water. Some anglers of the fly call it a prospector of sorts. This little gem of a bug, originally a caddis imitation, by the way, helps the fly fisherman in determining just what the trout may have an interest in on a particular day. Gives 'im some idea of what he should be using at the end of his tippet. Know what a tippet is, Jumbo?"

Big Bill had fallen asleep and most likely, not due to his acute interest. Poor Bill looked bored to death, his rosey face, expressionless. "Wake up, Moby Dick! You ain't sleepin' in my class! Just look at this luscious creation I've made with just a smidgen of thread and feathers!"

Bill opened his eyes, looked at Joe's delicious looking Adams fly and said, "Looks like somethin' that'd eat a hole in a good wool sweater, to me, Joseph!"

"Bill, this is what we of the purist fraternity refer to as an Adams. Kind of generic pattern sometimes angled as a mayfly imitation, when in reality it was originally designed by a Len Halladay of Michigan, to be a caddis imitation. Regardless, it catches trout when some flies won't, and it's a must for the flyfisher's fly box. Now, sit here behind the vise and ol' Joseph here'll show ya how to wrap your own." Joe looked at Big Bill's shaking fingers and whispered to himself, "What with fingers the size of pepperoni sticks, old Billy here would have a tough time with the dexterity needed to change a truck tire, let alone what he'll need to tie even a half-respectable fly..."

Joe got Bill all set up with the proper materials and enough instruction to keep him occupied a while then said, "Just sit there, Billy, try to relax yourself, take your time and try to copy the fly I've tied. I'll head on upstairs and warm us some of my potent cider."

"Okay little buddy, but heavy on the cinnamon, will ya, please?"

"Gotchya Porky, be back in a jif."

Poor sausage-fingered Bill. The sweat ran off his forehead like heavy rain off a dormer, as he labored over his "creation" in the vise. Upstairs, Joe could hear his beloved buddy singing, "...feathers and things and buttons and bows, for what you're gonna catch only the enema man knows!" Joe smiled with personal satisfaction. Thinking, what a guy Big Bill was...

After about ten minutes of Joe at the cider kettle and Big Bill at the tying vise, Joe returned to the basement. "Here ya go, Tons-Of-Fun! Ye old spiced cider from the magic, black kettle of Little-Joe-Heavy-on-the Cinnamon! Let us toast to your...Bill!" Joe's eyes bulged from their sockets like mini hot-air balloons, "What in the world is that humongous atrocity in my vise?"

"That there Little Buddy is Big Bill's first trout fly! Nice, hain't it?"

"Fly? Why Bill! Your first fly? That thing looks more like a pregnant ostrich for heaven's sake. Why that'd put a great white shark to swimming the opposite direction! Move over, let's lift that thing outta there and try to salvage a few pounds of my tying material!"

"I wouldn't move it yet, Joseph, hain't dry yet!"

"Bill, don't be worryin' about dry, why it'd take a week for all that head cement to dry! Sooner we get it out of there, the easier it'll be to save some of the materials!"

Joe began taking **THE FLY** from the vise. "Here now, little buddy, don't be a liftin' that beauty all by yourself! Let big ol' Billy here grab the other end."

Joe strained, careful not to aggravate an old hernia. "Just toss it over there in the corner, Bill, where no one'll trip over it! Ready? On three! One, two, heave!" **THE FLY** landed in the corner with a thud. Joe looked at it in amazement and began shaking his head back and forth. "Man Bill! Why someone sees that thing they'll think we scarfed up a road kill!"

"Geezooey, Little Buddy," Bill said looking down at the huge fly, "it is a big'un, hain't it? Kinda looks like our national bird a little, huh?" Bill laughed in that lovable, childish way of his, which always seemed to soften Joe's heart and make him forget his anger with Bill.

"Ha," Bill said, smiling at **THE FLY**, "If'n ol' Billy here tossed that thing in th' water, we'd limit out in no time! Daggone trout'd die of conclusion! Probably illegal though, huh, Joe?"

"Not conclusion, Bill – concussion, and never mind illegal, Bill. Let's just dismantle it and try to save *some* of those materials! C'mon now, help me drag it over there under the big light."

Big Bill began laughing as the two struggled with **THE MONSTER FLY**. "Why don't we just hollow the rascal out, Joe, and use it for a stylish fishin' boat!" He laughed uproariously, dropping his end of **THE FLY**. And Joe? He couldn't help but laugh along with Bill to the point where he weakened and fell to the basement floor... the purest evidence of how he really felt about his buddy, Bill.

Needless to say, Joe ended Bill's flytying lessons that evening, but promised to supply Bill with flies "henceforth." And come spring, Joe would hold to his promise, and teach Big Bill in the ways of the flyfisherman.

Ten-Mile Creek cut a watery trail through the picturesque mountains of southwestern Pennsylvania and was fed by numerous, small, springlike streams that trickled off the lush mountains, offering good oxygenated water and unlimited trout-fishing opportunities. Good water for the beginner, as it was wide enough to allow for the backcast and shallow enough in most sections to be easy to wade. Most pocket water was easily accessible and this was where Joe planned to "train" Big Bill.

"Bill, it'll be the pristine, meandering Ten-Mile we fish opening day. The perfect stream for your debut as a Purist of the fattest kind!"

Bill innocently asked, "Who's this Pristine-gal, she allow us to fish her crick?"

"Yeah, Bill, I got her permission..."

Bill cut Joe short. "I am read-deee, Partner. I have spent considerable bucks from my alooneyum cans I took t'th' recyclin' place, and, according to my wife, I've made some several dozen trips to ye' old flyshop. And, Joseefus, I have made purchases that'll make you proud, and your brotherly love for fat ol' Billy will only broaden. Joe, just wait until you cast your eyes upon Billy-boy's flyfishin' gear, ol' buddy!"

"Proud, Billy? Ya' mean like I was with your first fly? The remains of which still take up considerable cubic footage of my basement? Pleeeze, Bill, don't embarrass me with the brethren of flyfishers on opening day! Try to be a little conservative and civilized in this new endeavor, please! Don't be doing like you did on our first deer hunt together, when you wore so much fluorescent-orange I had to wear sunglasses around you before daylight!"

"Ta, ta, little brookie of B.B.I., settle yourself and trust in your student companion to bring your frail body and cold heart to the very threshold of pride on opening day! An enema man I may not be, but I will be *the* stylish one among the clan of flyfishermen for the opener!"

"Give ya this, Wil. Your English is improvin', but please, not enema, en**tomo**logy!"

Water was certain to be high and turbid for the opener, so Joe tied dozens of weighted wet flies, to include a few nymphs. This would allow the pair to get down, deep, where the trout would likely be feeding – where, in fact, they mostly feed anyway. Still, Joe worried about the effectiveness of flies for Day One. Too, the weather report called for, *"Mostly cloudy skies, with periods of light rain and gusty winds, up to 30-mph."*

Joe switched off the radio. "Brother!" he said to himself, "a windy first day is gonna make things tough, especially for poor old Billy. Hard enough for a skilled flyfisher to buck the winds with a fly..." Joe forever held Bill's best interests at heart and fervently wished for Bill's first-day success with the fly rod.

Joe thought again, "Heaven knows, I love the big dipstick, but if he gets frustrated with wind knots and all, he'll reduce his fly rod to mere high-tech chopsticks. Best I call a meeting of the ol' B.B.I. tonight."

Joe phoned Bill and the meeting was set for that night. Joe sat there seriously pondering the idea of teaching Big Bill to flyfish, of trying desperately to pound data into his ligneous-like head. To him, without old Bill along, his constant companion, outings would be at best phlegmatic and spiritless. Bill was a joy to spend time with anywhere, and Joe so often referred to Bill as his "Memory-Maker." His partner, and a day spent without the company of Bill was just that – a day spent.

He'd always felt this strong responsibility for Bill, and, pain that he was sometimes, he nonetheless had a way about him that made Joe's days afield (however fruitless) memorable days, worthwhile and wholesome. "I'm darned lucky to have the old poop," Joe thought as he sat at his kitchen table.

Joe's missus walked in, interrupting his thoughts: "Are you asleep, Joseph?"

"No, no! I was just sitting here thinking how fortunate I really am to have old Billy as a partner."

"Yes, you are! And if it weren't for bad luck, you'd have none! Now, why don't you go to the sofa and take a little nap?"

"Okay," Joe said, yawning, "but how's about your thawing out some of those mincemeat cookies for tonight? There's an emergency meeting of the B.B.I. tonight, and Big Bill always brings along a full appetite!"

"Best we hide the doggie treats right now, then!" said Joe's missus. "He ate a whole box the last time you turkeys had a 'meeting'!"

The meeting convened and Big Bill was given hours of last-minute instructions for his flyfishing debut. Joe made Bill pronounce 'entomology' at least fifty times, praying all the while he wouldn't say "enema-ology" in front of Joe's friends, especially those who read his outdoor column week in and week out. "It'd blow my reputation to the wind," he thought.

After the meeting, Bill began his rummaging through the kitchen cupboards. "Where in devil's name ya' hidin' the doggie treats, these days, Joseefus?"

"Under the sink there, big guy, but go easy on 'em, or you'll spend the entire day in the Porta-Potty down at old Ten-Mile!" Joe laughs, and Bill joins in.

"Ha! Ya might be better off with me in the one-holer than on the crick!"

The morning of the opener dawned windy as radio promised. Bill, as usual, arrived two hours earlier than instructed. When Joe opened the door at his knocking, there stood Big Bill in the garb of the ultimate flyfisherman, looking as though he'd bought and was now wearing every item Orvis had in their warehouse!

"Mornin', Billy! What is that stench?"

"Stench? What's 'stench'?" Bill questioned with that childish, puzzled look which always melted Joe's "tough" heart.

"Okay, Bill, stink, s-t-i-n-k, stink! What is that stink?"

"Oh, that? Probably comin' from where I burned this here vest in the back while tryin' t'iron on the duct tape."

"Duct tape? For what?"

"Well," Bill said, "I hadda sew two vests together since the catalogs didn't have 'em in m'size, and not being much of a sewin' man, I kinda had t'tidy it all up and cover the stitchin' with duct tape. Daggone stuff don't take much to ironin', but aside from that, Little Buddy, how's your ol' pardner lookin'?"

"Fine, Bill, ya look just fine! I could probably put a down payment on the Hearst castle with less money than you musta spent on all that stuff! And how, may I ask, are you ever going to remove all those flies from your hat, even though I tied all we'll ever need this season?"

"Like that arrangement, do ya? Why, there's four or five dozen of them babies pinned in there. Got 'em at the Dollar Department Store for ninety-nine cents on the dozen. Ol' Billy here is a-ready as a Freddy and 'um gonna knock 'em dead today, Little Buddy!"

"Bill, the smell of that vest alone ought to knock 'em dead! C'mon, let's get rolling!"

At the stream: "Okay, Bill, listen up. I'll be upstream from you just a'ways. Work those flies deep and strip line to prevent slack, so you'll see or feel the strikes. Fish 'em downstream and across like I taught ya and mend your line when it starts to belly on you, okay? And, Bill, pleeeeeze don't be dropping that hat into the water or we'll be arrested for chumming! Got it?"

"Yeah, I got it, Joe, except what do you mean 'mend'? You can see by this vest I hain't much of a mender!"

"Just fish, Bill, and good luck."

Joe watched Big Bill at every opportunity. The wind was playing havoc with the leader and after just a couple of hours, and one morsel of a rainbow, Joe decided they'd better pack it in for the day.

"Hey, Billy! Let's hang 'er up, Big Buddy," Joe said as he approached Bill's position downstream. "This wind is a killer! How'd you do?"

Bill smiled that priceless smile of his and answered, "Shoot, Little Buddy, been done for nigh on fifteen minutes now. Got me eight 'bows lickety split! How's 'bout you?"

Joe said, "Just got one rainbow about the size of your little finger, Bill. That's about it." Joe's eyes watered as he examined Bill's leader, which had back-to-back knots from butt to tippet. "Bill, look at your leader, fer cryin' out loud! How'd'ya ever limit out using that thing? Looks like some crazed Boy Scout went on a rampage trying to get his knot-tying merit badge!"

"Why, Joseefus, I had a fine instructor, did I not – get it, *knot*?"

"Yeah, Billy, I get it. Now I think we'd best head for the Coffee Palace and call it a mornin', okay?"

As they sat sipping coffee, they reviewed the morning's activities. "Ya know, Chubby line chucker, I'm right proud of you!" Joe said, patting Bill's mountainous shoulder. "Why, a limit of trout first time flyrodding? That *is* great! Tell me, Billy, what pattern were you using all morning?"

"I think," Bill said, removing his fly-filled hat and scratching his head, "it was a Royal Roachman, Joe. I h'ain't real sure now, since the daggone fly is still in that last trout I landed. I'll find it when I clean 'em up later an' let ya know."

"Bill," Joe said, giggling, "read my lips. Say, Royal *Coachman*."

As the pair were ready to leave the Palace, Joe reached into his pocket and came to realize he'd forgotten his wallet. "Doggone it, Billy, I was gonna pick up the tab, but it appears I left my wallet at home. Got any cash with you?"

"Sure I do, Tiny Tightwad, sure do!" Bill reached into the depths of his sewn-together vests and pulled forth a handful of change. A rather muddied tin fell to the floor, which caused the lip to jar open. Out onto the linoleum floor spilled a huge gob of tangled, very juicy-looking and lively red worms! Joe, in total disbelief, eyed the red worms as though they were toxic waste, then looked sternly into Bill's squinting, guilt-ridden blue eyes.

"Think it was a Royal Roachman, huh, Big Boy?"

Bill, near frantic from fear of being strongly reprimanded, said, "Listen, Joe. I lost ever' fly you gave me, in that big old tree behind me this mornin', and I couldn't free the ones stuck in m'hat. Why, that wind was horrendous, and I couldn't get my flyline to do anything right! I just hadta use the worms so you wouldn't think all those lessons ya gave me were for nuttin'. I wanted t'make ya proud of old Billy, so I tied on a snelled number eight and fished my worms. Caught 'em all on the flyrod, though. Please don't be ticked with me, Little Buddy, I was just tryin' to make ya proud of the way ya taught me to handle the flyrod, is all!"

"Bill, let's go to the truck!" Bill followed Joe to the truck like a geisha girl, fearing what might be about to transpire ....

After they'd gotten outside, Joe looked squarely into Bill's big, frightened eyes. He removed Bill's new flyrod from its perch inside the truck and, sighing, said, "Billy, my friend, you have done a grave injustice to this beautiful flyrod. But then, on the other hand, you have fared well in the face of tremendous adversity. That wind was very tough to contend with today. Indeed it was! But, still, William, that's no reason to dishonor a rod as fine as a Hexagraph! Imagine how it would be hurting if it in fact had a heart!"

"What do ya mean, Little Buddy?"

"What I mean, Bill, is this: there is a strong, well-adhered-to tradition among the purists of flyfishermen, and your shame should forever grieve and haunt you!"

Half-smiling, half-bewildered, Bill asked, "What tradition, Joe?"

"Why, ya big dummy, you got mud all over the cork handle, leaving it there for all to see, that's what tradition! Folks'll know you were wormin' with your flyrod! Now, let's get home and clean it off before someone of the fraternity sees it!"

Big Bill's eyes swelled with tears of relief and gratitude. He loved his B.B.I. leader, with his understanding way. "Yeah, Joe. Yeah! Let's go clean 'er up, and, Joe?"

"Yes, Bill?"

"I wanna make you a promise here an' now! I'm gonna become the best flyfisherman you ever know'd. Even better than that Hefty Clay fella, Joe!"

"It's Kreh, Bill, and Lefty Kreh, not Hefty!"

"Whatever, Joe, I'm gonna get good at it, just you watch. And ya know, all I gotta do is stay off the cricks on windy days and get me a handle on that enema-ology stuff!"

"Right, Billy. And you may just want to remember to always clean off the cork handle if you're going to expect folks to believe you caught your trout on a Royal Roachman!"

AUTHOR'S NOTE: This time and the men in the story represent an ethereal memory I so very often summon when Life is, at the moment, not so kind. When perhaps despair is, sadly, more abundant than happiness. For example, I wrote this old piece which was first published (and written) back in the early 80's, during the heartbreaking days of the Oklahoma bombing news coverage and after I, myself, covered that story for two different newspapers. At that time, and for months afterwards, I was one angry, unhappy, revenge-seeking American man. . . The story helped, however little, but still, it's one of my favorites and sharing it fills my heart to where little might "drain" it. This, then, is the reason I chose to include it in this collection; for your enjoyment?

As a youngster, my greatest memories were those given me by my grandfather, Joe Parry I. We've all heard the old story about the "pot of gold at the end of the rainbow." As far back as I remember, I felt Grandfather **was** my personal "pot of gold." One of life's burning propensities for me has forever been to share some of this marvelous man with the world. I did it to some extent as a boy, but then Grandfather died when I was a soldier in the U.S. Army. I was 18 and able to come home and carry him to his place in the Earth.

Now he's somewhere else, hopefully better, so I must share just this little bit of him with you here. However, no words by any writer, certainly one as pedestrian as Joe II, could capture the gold in this old timer's great heart. . .


"One Man's Fox"


My father was a lenient cuss back in the early 50's. Bless his heart; he felt a man should know more about modified and full than of Lewis and Clark. And I did. . .

The 50's were times when an intimate knowledge of choke patterns and wisely selected shot sizes meant meat in the winter larder; more important to the men in our family than any historical expedition. Harvest time and canning season ran a tail-sniffing second only to Christmas when it came to excitement and celebration. Simple living, shotguns and survival were words to virtually live by. And though times were tough, they remained unpretentious and the quality of everyday life back then was unequaled.

As a youngster of the 50's, one had precious little time for leisure or recreation. There was recreation alright, but what we considered fun or enjoyable then, may by today's standards, be labeled "work."

There was a lengthy trapline to work, coal to shovel, wood to split, hides to scrape and stretch and a father's heating and plumbing shop to tend in the town of Greensburg, PA, to name but a few! Recreation or leisure in those days might have been lying before the fireplace watching the odd flickering reflection of flames dancing on the pages of an arithmetic book. This was about as close to recreation as the times would allow, and, insofar as entertainment goes, it really wasn't all that bad. Flame dancing had a way of stirring the dreamer in a kid and if a kid of the fabulous 50's measured dreams in terms of currency, each of us was wealthy. . .

This youngster's dreams were of bone-handled sheath knives, high-lacing leather boots that kissed the bottom of the knees, red and black wool-plaid hunting shirts and jackets, not having to wear those cloddy galoshes to school and shotguns, actually all guns, but smoothbores in particular. At least those shotgun types that didn't outweigh the family dog (we always had big dogs!) or those able to exceed the shooting range of a 105-Howitzer!

Grandfather, whom everyone, including me, called Pap, owned such a gun, one which was synonymous with the adjective, "sleek." A Fox Sterlingworth in 16-bore. A piece of simple weaponry that came to the shoulder with unnoticeable effort at the urging of a single brain cell. One of those rare shotguns that one could truly, "just point!" The spray from the business end seemed, then, (and now!)

magical. The old Fox was as elegant and as slim as a winter weasel, as solid as the safes of Switzerland. And the only gun in Pap's humble arsenal—used to kill everything from blackbirds to whitetails.

I recall a deer season long before the time I was part of the gang, when Pap killed an eight-point buck with a single shot from the Fox. Launching a "punkinball" from such a gun seemed sacrilegious, like asking the Pope to a beer party, but still, it was an impressive accomplishment. . . I can hear Pap saying, "Boy oh boy, Joey, that old buck went down like someone hit him on the coconut with a sledge hammer!" Pap was from the "old country," and every head, animal's or human's, was a coconut.

My childhood arsenal was simple. I had but a timeless Daisy Red Ryder BB gun. But it became highly notorious in our country neighborhood, perhaps even more than the buntline carried by one infamous Wyatt Earp? Neighbors referred to it as ". . .the little devil's deadly Daisy." I just called her Daisy. And to this day, it's the only gun I've ever seen that shot two trajectories; one which pushed the BB earthward in short order and the other which drove it, drastically, to the right. However, in time, I learned to make up for Daisy's inadequacies.

My trapline gun, which actually belonged to my father, was an old, acne-ridden Steven's single-shot .22. I did have a sleek back pocket companion of awesome power: A slingshot I'd crafted from a slick "Y" branch I'd found in a neighbor's garage. But yes, that was it. My arsenal extraordinaire; deer rifles such as Dad's .300 Savage lever and the smooth-handling Fox doubles such as Pap's were guns that fired my nightly dreams—only!

At twelve, I was given a beautiful (cosmetically only!) German side-by-side shotgun choked "Clark & Clark." Or full and full like many shotguns of European persuasion. The barrels on the German gun were all of 34-inches long and the chokes tighter than the north-end of a south-bound field mouse! Pinpoint accuracy was mandatory (not the norm with a scattergun) and if I planned to eat (which we always did!) what I shot, I **had** to make a headshot. . .

Pap, Dad, (Dad later became "Pap") and Uncle Buck used to chuckle in such a mischievous manner, it made my ears turn red every time we went hunting and I toted the old German gun. Pap would sympathize: "It's sinful to bring up a hunting son with a shotgun that shoots a tighter 'group' than a deer rifle!" But, as nerve-testing time went by in the pheasant swamps and quail fields, I became pretty handy with the old German, not to mention that I, very likely, became the sole, living reason Remington-Peters' stocks split several times? Why I'd bought enough shells with my trapline bounty, they may have, at one time, written me some sort of endorsement contract? Perhaps even a toll-free hotline number straight to their master loader's cubicle?

In later years, I was honored with an opportunity to shoot with the famous cowboy, Roy Rogers. We'd moved to California just prior to my graduation year and lived but a few miles from him. And a finer gentleman I've yet to meet!

I managed to outshoot Roy in two rounds of trap, using the old German. Roy, in that gentle, soft drawl he had back then said, "Why, I've never seen anyone wait quite so long to smoke a clay bird!" I told him if I didn't wait until the clays were almost in the neighboring county, I'd likely miss them; that the old thing shot a terribly tight pattern. That day, if I recall, Roy and I sat on his Chatsworth, California ranch and he asked me whether I'd sell him the shotgun. He loved it. "Roy, I'd love you to have it, believe me, but my father liberated it from a Nazi concentration camp (Buchenwald) and I just couldn't let it go." He, of course, understood, but still asked if he could shoot a round or two of clays with it. And shoot he did! He shot that old German shotgun better than anyone ever did. He was and is and forever shall be, "The King of Cowboys!" A personal hero of mine for countless years. . .

One evening as I was feverishly sweating over a dozen or so chilled muskrats (when they're cold, getting their skin off is akin to peeling porcelain off a sink top!), Pap stopped by. He sat quietly on the old cider barrel for the longest time, smoking one of those Italian stogies which smelled not better than fresh water buffalo droppings!

"Joey," he finally said, "you're growing into one fine young man. You're a hard worker. And I suppose (he spoke broken Italian!) you feel your daddy and I don't recognize this in you all the time? But we do, Son, and I want to let you know that one of these days, real soon probably, old Pap-Pap is going to give you his Fox. But only when I'm sure you've become a responsible man, and earned the right to carry such a fine gun. The Fox, you know, is one of the world's greatest shotguns?"

I lit up like a 30-minute road flare! "Pap," I said, "I'd love to own a Fox just like yours, but not **your** Fox!" Still, he insisted it was mine when and if I proved myself responsible and mature. And, as I look back, I think I would have duked it out with the great Rocky Marciano, bare-knuckled, for that old Fox!

A few days later, Pap came out to the house and decided to burn off the buffalo grass in a section where he planned to plant next spring. Our field was about 2-acres. We took up our rakes and shovels and Pap methodically set the field afire. But moments later, the wind kicked up and the field began to burn wildly—out of control!

We smacked at flames for all we were worth, Pap even resorting to using his sweaty, old shirt but our efforts seemed (and were!) hopeless. Panic came into play, for there was no way we could contain this fire ourselves. And we realized it in very short order. If the fire had spread to a neighbor's grove of blue spruce, we'd have been in serious trouble. Our neighbor was attorney Fred Seymour.

The nearest water source was a hose bib on the side of our house, all of 100-yards away! Our hose was 50-feet long, or worse, 250-feet short! My mind raced, my heart pounded mercilessly. Then I remembered. The neighbor's pool was still full of water. I ran to the garage, grabbed two, five-gallon buckets we used for apple picking and raced toward the pool. Heaven knows how many trips to and from the pool I made, carrying water buckets, but not long after say, umpteen-hundred sprints, Pap and I had the fire completely under control. I was exhausted. Imagine, a 120-pounder running for the better part of a half an hour carrying some 80-pounds per sprint?

Pap, too, was exhausted. We just sat there in silence watching millions of little smoke curls heading upward from the smoldering field. Pap suddenly looked over at me and began laughing. So heartily, it caused my laughter to kick in! "I just wish you could have seen yourself running back and forth with those big water buckets! Pap was so afraid you were going to trip over your tongue. Why, your arms are probably six-inches longer now!" He's borderline hysterical now! "Why, if you ever grow into them, you'll be able to play for the Harlem Globe Trotters!" I was tired and just looked over and into his smiling eyes and chuckled.

Pap continued: "You've done a fine thing, Joey. As funny as it is right now, it was an emergency and you kept your head and took care of it. That fire could've turned into a big problem. You've done real well, son, real well. How foolish Pap-Pap was to set such a large section on fire with just the two of us to take care of it. By golly, old Pap is proud of you."

Hunting season came and I, again, toted the old German to the swamp and fields. And yes, once again everyone got their laughs about my having to use the "scatter-rifle." Pap spoke in my defense: "Regardless of how we poke fun at Joey, he's become a darned fine wingshot with that double and not one of us has shot doubles on grouse like he did. Let the boy have some peace. . ." I doubt I would have survived my teenage years without him, without his loving support. Sure, I had my other crosses to bear, like everyone else, but the German double was indeed the worst thorn in my posterior. . .

Come November 13th, I'd turn 16. That meant a driver's license, drive-in movies, cruising Greensburg's Main Street and a cheerleader riding shotgun for me—and **with** me!

I had plenty of money saved from pelt sales and just prior to turning 16, I planned to buy a '48 Chevy coupe from a friend. Dad opposed the transaction and I tried for all I was worth to convince him that just because he heard it needed an entire exhaust system, four tires, wrist-pins, an engine and a heater core was not reason enough to prohibit my buying it! The deal, of course, never transpired. . .

November 13 was going much like any other day. Up at 5 a.m., check the trapline, store the muskrats in my burlap bounty bag, change boots to shoes, catch the schoolbus, spend eight hours giving various teachers gray hair, flirt with Kathy Elder, work in Dad's plumbing & heating shop for heaven knew how long, go home, skin out the muskrats, eat supper, do homework, then? Go to bed! Whew! Long sentence, longer day. . .

That night however, wasn't your normal 1958 evening. After supper, Pap came over and asked Dad to go somewhere in his old Jeep Wagoneer. I was asked to "guard the cake" until they returned and to get my homework done.

Soon, Pap's Jeep came up the drive and moments later, they came into the house and asked my stepmother and siblings, Cheryl, Frankie and Kelly, to follow them outside. "Joey, lead the way." Pap said. As we all marched toward the door, Dad switched on the floods to light the driveway area.

As I looked out onto the drive, I saw a shiny 1951 Chevy coupe sitting there, a Deluxe model in two-door! I looked questioningly back toward Dad. "Yep, yours," is all he said, nodding his head. The Chevy was mine. Mouth open, jaw agape, I walked toward the car, then trotted the remaining 10-yards or so. I touched virtually every surface on it as though it were a Rolls Royce and seconds later noticed it had a low, rear tire. Pap said, "Don't you worry, Joey, there's a new tire pump in the trunk!" He tossed me the keys.

I opened the trunk and there, inside, was one of our five-gallon apple buckets with something sticking out of it. I reached and pulled out the barrel half of Pap's Fox

Sterlingworth, then the stock assembly. I peeked out from inside the trunk in Pap's direction, then held up the barrel section wearing a quizzical look. "That's yours too, Joey. Happy Birthday, Son! And that bucket you just took it from is what helped earn you the Fox for your very own!"

I know I didn't cry that night as I cuddled up in bed, next to the Fox. Boys of the fifties never cried or at least never fetched up to so doing. I do know, however, I wanted to, for that Fox meant more to me than the '51 Chevy or any gift I'd ever before received. And I remember the feeling I had that night as though it were this morning. My Fox, why it was (is) so sleek, my stepmother never even noticed it beneath my covers that night: November 13, 1958.

The Fox to this day hangs in our home. I've given it to my son, Justin, but we sort of share ownership. It looks as well or better than it did that long ago night. Justin, however, felt it should be retired but still, every once in a while when we'd get serious about sharing a brace of grouse for dinner, one of us will take it down and get the job done with the magic, old Fox. Maybe once a year. . .

One late night, while in the mood for handling the Fox, I took it down wearing that automatic smile it always brought to my face. I looked it over affectionately and shot a few imaginary grouse that have a welcome habit of flushing from a corner in our living room; my way of shooting doubles anytime I wish. . .

This late-night ambition along with an ardent need to fondle the old gun, soon had me rubbing it down with Liquid Gold and light-coating the liquid-steel barrels with Hoppe's No. 9. As I sat there rubbing in the Gold, I noticed the pistol-grip cap was a bit loose. I removed it with a screwdriver to see what the problem was. And there in the walnut, hidden all these years by the cap, were the crudely carved initials, "J.P."

Pap's name, of course, was Joe Parry too. And my son's initials are J.P. His middle name being Joseph. So, I figured Pap had it all planned long ago? He was magical and very wise and clearly, to all who knew him, the greatest man they'd ever known. . .

And I suppose what hurts most, is the fact that the Fox's original owner isn't around these parts anymore. And he was the man who made a man of me by giving me a very special Fox 16-bore, for he said, "This will teach you great responsibility, Joey." It has done that and so much more. I feel sure Pap knew I'd one day have a son of my own to whom I'd ultimately give the Fox. I've done that, for he's a fine young man; responsible, and a better son doesn't exist.

I also feel sure he loves and appreciates the old gun as much as I did when I got it. He's told me and yes, he knows the story of how I came to get it. He's very appreciative too, of not having to get it the way I did in the 50's, for he's said, "Geez, Pop, you aren't gonna be setting any fields on fire are you, you never did grow into your arms and I don't want any part of having arms with which I can scratch my knees without having to bend over just a little. . ."

"No fires, Son, no fires. Just that which burns inside of me for you, your great-grandfather and that old Fox which now belongs to one man. . ."

## "Something About A Gun"

It was William Shakespeare, I believe, who said, "one touch of nature makes the whole world kin." I doubt, however, that he was a hunter. If so, he may have added, "There's something about a gun that unites hunting men like brothers."

An elderly gent lived down near the end of our woodland road, in a humble little home that almost seemed like something out of a storybook. Every time one of us passed the other's home we'd wave, but that was pretty much all there was to our friendship. Yard work kept each of us busy throughout the summer. Winters were too miserable for either one of us, old as we are, to get out and about – unless it was deer season, as that in and of itself seems to warm the blood of most predatory men. Adrenaline flow carries strength to our aging legs, hips and backs, so that come the season for whitetails, we ancient ones appear as teenage athletes sauntering up the sides of the Endless Mountains. And hunting season is what finally brought the old man and me together.

I was nestled in a scooped-out section of the mountain I call Big Leek Hill. It was opening day of deer season, albeit unseasonably warm, almost shirt-sleeve weather. Early in the morning, nine whitetails tiptoed by; a small buck in the scampering group was no more than 25 yards away. I was carrying a new Marlin Model 444P in

444-caliber, which at that distance would have killed the buck with nearly a ton and a half of energy. I chose to pass on this first little buck of the new season. At about 11 a.m., I headed down the mountain to the house for lunch. I'd already passed on the second buck of the day, at around 10:30. I was holding out for a dream buck I'd seen near what I refer to as "the lonely hemlock." I rough-scored him through binoculars one morning as he chased off another buck from the does he was following, and figure he was of 165 Boone & Crockett points. I had called my son Justin out to have a look, and the words from his mouth were, "Oh my gosh, Pop, he's incredible. Biggest I've ever seen. How about you?"

"I'd say so, son, and you know very well that I've lived at all four corners of the lower 48. Why, the 8-point he chased away from his does was bigger than any mulie I've ever taken. I've seen deer with antler bases nine inches around, and the 8-point he chased off was all of that, likely bigger. High tines, too, most about eight, maybe nine inches and straight as sticks. Two incredible whitetails in one morning is almost too much for this old man's heart to take."

Justin asked softly, "Ya gonna kill 'im if ya get the chance, Pop?"

"Won't know, Partner, until the moment presents itself, if indeed it does. That buck didn't get as big as he is by being careless. Nor did the 8-point. I'd sure love the opportunity, though. Just to see them during buck season would be reward enough, but I never really know what I'm gonna do until the time comes. Reckon I've always been a fickle old poop."

Walking down the mountainside, I spotted a speck of orange at a location I call "the funnel." It's a place where the deer almost have to cross to get to another mountain's cover. I detoured out of curiosity. I wanted to know who this hunter was.

As I got closer, I noticed a scruff of snow-white hair sticking out from under his Elmer Fudd-like hunting cap. It was my elderly acquaintance from the end of our road, whose surname I knew to be Mancini. Not wanting to frighten him, because I felt he, like me, may be hard of hearing, I made the *psst* sound. It came out well. The old-timer turned toward me, smiled what I felt to be the warmest smile I'd ever seen from a man and softly said, "howdy."

I smiled in response and whispered "Mornin' neighbor. Seen anything worthwhile?"

He spoke with a broken and heartwarming Italian accent. An accent I grew up with as I, too am of Italian descent, and my grandfather spoke broken English. His accent, his way of pronouncing English words, made him all the more lovable, and hearing Mr. Mancini was déjà vu extraordinaire.

Grandfather passed away when I was in basic training back in 1960. I got home to attend his funeral, but I miss him terribly. He was my hero. In fact, it was he, my father and a favorite uncle, Buck Budd, who introduced me to hunting back in 1954. I even had a few years' experience carrying the men's harvest and no gun and, as I said, there's something about a gun that brings men together intimately.

"I no see a da one ting cept da doggonit does all mornin'. And dis a new gun a mine, justa bought, anna first new ting I ever have for to hunt wit donna shoot wort beans. Why you sa neighbor, no?"

"Your neighbor I am, Mr. Mancini. So, you've seen nothing with antlers, huh?"

"Nading, young man, nading 'tall. Justa squirrels a digging da nuts anna couple bigga, fatta does."

"How about coming home for lunch with me, Mr. Mancini? Perhaps we can work out an afternoon strategy, and if we're lucky, maybe one of us will score on one of the two big bucks I saw earlier this fall."

"Shore ting. Say, whattsa you name anyways?"

"Joe. Joe Parry. But long ago, before my grandfather changed it, our family name was Parisi. I'm Italian, too."

"Well daggonit, attsa nice ting to know. I taught so. You have gooda Romano nose. Giuseppe isa you name in Italiano, ya know it?"

I said that I did, and he got up and we headed for the house for lunch.

"Whattsa dis a ting you calla shratasee?"

"It's strategy, Mr. Mancini."

"Pleasa, Joe, donnta calla me a Mister Mancini, my name a isa Luigi in Italiano."

"Okay, Louie it is. Now tell me, Louie, what's the problem with your rifle? You mentioned it doesn't shoot worth beans?"

"Daggonit ting shootsa holes all over da paper targets an not all a dem inna da bullseye. I dunna whattsa matter witta daggonit sing. You tinka you can fix, no?"

"Well, maybe, Louie, maybe. We'll see what the problem is when we get to the barn."

He looked at me through proud hazel eyes in which I could see me own reflection and said, "Ya know, Giuseppe, dissa gun a mine is da first ting I ever boughta myself new. I never hadda monies tilla dissa year, an I was alla cited about it until I shotta da doggonit sing. Well she no shoots a too good. Make sa me sad a little bits, you know it?"

"I believe I know how you feel, Louie, but I think I already know what the problem is. Let me see it for a minute."

It was a gorgeous .308 Winchester in the Classic Model 70 Featherweight. The stock was well-figured and breathtaking. Unusual for a production rifle out of the box. "Well, Louie, this is one of the finest guns a man could own. Called the rifleman's rifle because of its outstanding reputation and durability under tough conditions without problems occurring. It should shoot well at almost any range. Let's look at it when we get to the house."

"Tanka you, Joe, tanka you veddy, veddy much. I'a justa hope itsa nading a too daggon bad?"

At the house we ate sourdough bread, cucumber salad and huge squares of left-over lasagna, then washed it down with a non-alcoholic white wine, chilled for a week. He thanked me dozens of times for lunch, to the point where I was all but embarrassed. We went to the den and I took out my gun kit. I took the action from the bed of the stock, and sure enough, there were several pressure marks. Also, I had a suspicion that someone had tightened the wrong action screw first. Always, but always, however trivial it may sound, tighten the rear screw first. And bear down on it until you feel the beginnings of a hernia. This makes a world of difference in how well a rifle shoots.

I have a friend, Butch Murray from Erie, who bought a Sako in .243 that the owner claimed just won't shoot well at all. Butch brought it to me after having paid only $150 for it. I took it out of the stock, checked for pressure markings. There were none at all.

"Nothing wrong here, Butch," I said, "but let's try this one thing I learned long ago from my Uncle Buck Budd."

I placed the barrel back into the stock, placed the action screws in their respective holes and proceeded to bear down hard on the rear screw. I then finished tightening the front screw, and we took it to the range that afternoon. Butch had fired it earlier, and his 3-shot group measured nearly 12 inches, however, the Sako shot 1-inch groups, after the adjustments.

I sanded out the pressure marks on Louie's Winchester and smoothed it off with fine steel wool, then carefully set the barrel and action back into its wooden bed. I bore down on the rear action screw until the veins in my forehead looked vividly reminiscent of purple night crawlers. We fired the rifle at my range in my back field. At 50 yards it hit about a quarter-inch high.

Louie said, "Sure, Joe, da ting will putta wonna shot prettie gooda, but a number two, tree anna four will go a every daggonit place. Speshally atta hundred yardsa."

I decided to use one of my hand loaded 165-grain boattail Barnes XLC coated bullet loads. This is what I used in the first round, and in my .30-06 Ruger, these precision bullets group an inch and under all day if, indeed, I do my part. I set up a new target at 100 yards and fired three of the hand loaded cartridges. The shots formed a perfect triangle just about ¾ of an inch.

"Owl be-a doggonit. I neber seena nading like at, Joe." Louie said.

We then headed for Big Leek Mountain where I'd secretly hoped and prayed Louie would get a shot at one of the two bucks. I placed him in a good spot and said, "Those cartridges I gave you, Louie will put down anything in North America. Just put the crosshairs where you want 'em and shoot." I told him I'd circle the mountain and, I hoped, move one of the big bucks out of the thick stuff and into his shooting lane.

"Ya tink da doggonit ting a comma dis way, Joe?"

"Gonna be a lot of fruitless walking if one doesn't, Louie. Just sit real tight for about two hours. Give me time to circle the mountain. I feel pretty certain at least one of them is holed up in that acre or two of mulitflora rose on the other side, and if I flush one, he's almost certain to come over the knoll here and head for the thicket behind the college. Good luck, Louie. See ya in a couple hours."

He whispered, "Ya know, Giuseppe, I never shota deer inna all da years since I come from da ol' country. I woulda love ta do dat doggonit ting justa one time before I die."

I worked my way slowly around the mountain, and not 30 minutes after I'd left Louie, I heard what I thought was his .308. Hoping so much that he had a buck, I continued my drive and returned to find Louie sitting on a big fallen log. In front of him lay the largest 8-point buck I'd seen in 44 years of hunting. "Hey, Louie, you got one of the big ones."

When the old man looked up at me without uttering a sound, his face was as white as an Ivory soap bar. "Hey ya, Joe. Yep, I gottsa him alright, but I don't know whatta do now. I never take a gutsa out of one before."

"Don't fret, Louie my friend. I'll take care of that."

"Boy a boy," Louie said, "You like a ma guide service man. Firsta ya take a care ma new rifle, den you clean uppa ma bigga buck, da first one I ever shoota, an I gotta paya you soma ting, Giuseppe."

"Louie, just knowing you, being your neighbor and friend is pay enough for me. Besides, you remind me of my long gone grandfather. Never mind the pay stuff."

Louie mentioned he would have the deer mounted. We tagged then dragged the deer about 1,000 yards to Louie's house, and I helped him skin and butcher it. He showed me around his cozy little home and sadly mentioned that his only son was killed in a helicopter crash in Vietnam. "I sure missa him, Guiseppa. I no be a da same since he go to heaven, ya know?"

No, I didn't know. No parent should live to see their child die, and I had two children at home. It made me think of the unthinkable.

Louie and I became close friends that winter. He was, aside from my grandfather, the kindest, most gentle, lovable, sincere and honest man I ever knew. He often called me his son, Giuseppe Parisi. It touched me in a way I've never been touched. Then one dreary afternoon he read one of my older *Game News* stories, "On War and Whitetails" in the August 1995 issue, and afterward phoned me to come over for a visit, teas and Italian anisette cookies. I could tell from the tone of his voice he was a bit melancholy, perhaps thinking about his dead son. Nevertheless, I threw on my vest and went to his home.

At the door, Louie laughed and said, "Comma inna you besta guide a service man." I laughed and said I might send him a bill yet if he didn't stop thanking me for what happened during buck season.

"Ya know, Joe, I no live too much a long. I like you ta know, I gonna leave you soma sing. Somma ting veddy, veddy nice when I go to hunta witta God. I hope you like."

I spent the better part of the afternoon with him. His wife, Mary, sat with us, quietly knitting him a sweater with huge pockets for "all the daggonit junks I carries arounda."

Mary had mentioned Louie's emphysema and heart condition, and sure enough, two weeks later, grand old Louie passed away on the sofa, in his cozy, little cottage, with his newly knitted sweater on. God knew I would miss him, his bright, warm smile, his laughter at the slightest humor and those warm moments when I knew he saw his own dead son in me.

I went to the viewing but couldn't, for whatever reason, attend his funeral. To my heart, that's too final to conceive. I watched as they lifted his copper casket into the hearse, went to my car and headed for church to light a few candles in his honor. It was a long, tough day, and henceforth it would be one long, rather lonely life without Louie's laughter, warm smiles and friendship.

Later that month Louie's wife phoned. "Joe, do you have time to come by the house for a few minutes?" Certainly I did, and I left within five minutes of her call. She opened the back door and asked if I would sit and drink the tea and eat the anisette cookies she had prepared, and that she'd be back in a minute. When she came back in she had a long box that appeared brand new. "Louie left you this deer head, Joe, and whatever's in this box."

Tears welled up in my old eyes, for I already knew what the box held. I wasn't, however, prepared for the letter attached to Louie's once-used Winchester. "Giuseppe, I loved you like my own son. I wanna you ta have dissa here gun anna buck head. I know you take a gooda care. Bless you, Joe. Love, Louie."

I left the house in a quiet mood, thinking, indeed, there's something about a gun. Something I was very thankful for. Tanka you Louie. Tanka you, veddy veddy much.

AUTHOR'S NOTE: This story was inspired by a photo sent to me by whom countless thousands feel is the greatest outdoor writer (although he never liked the title "outdoor writer.") of our century, one Gene Hill. He mailed me a photo from a time he was on safari in Africa showing him kneeling next to a massive sable.

## "Bwana Punda:
## A Hunter's Love Story"

His love of hunting began in 1951 but began to peak just after June of '72. And, for the record, it was after one simple, innocent, somewhat noncommittal kiss. A gesture of definite amorous meaning which comes very hard from the lips of a remarkably tough outdoorsman.

Just writing the word, "kiss" here comes after a lengthy reluctant period of contemplation, during which he scoured his one million word synonym finder for an appropriate substitute. As evidenced above, he couldn't find one less mushy or more masculine since "smooch" has little – make that **no** place in his life or vocabulary, regardless of how pedestrian both may indeed be. . .

The infamous kiss aforementioned (reluctantly!) was placed upon the lips of this outdoor writer's wife, but before she was "his wife," some 24 years ago. To him it meant, simply, "Geesh, your lips are pretty and soft," but to her? Obviously, it meant, (again, to write this now, he's fighting the sentence with great gusto), "You must love me and you must want to marry me?" And though he may not have meant exactly that at the time, he eventually did marry his lady friend of one year. Enter here, June 1, 1973. And shortly thereafter, his love of hunting intensified to the point where he took it more seriously than a brain surgeon might take operating on his very own four-pound gray mass! Now that's focused concentration!

Confinement with any one person can do things to the mind, to the quality of mental health, and has this prodding effect akin to being stuck in the posterior with a dull ice pick. Left dangling there until something could be done about it, this man chose to hunt everything the game commission would allow and at any time of year.

Now it's important to note, this hunter/outdoor writer decided in 1980 to cultivate a moustache which he still wears as a sort of symbol, a badge of courage, a status-quo, actually, among his writing peers. And, because of his relentless and constant hunting, being gone from dawn until dusk each and every day, sometimes dawn to dawn, his wife of now 7 years never noticed the bristly growth until about Christmas of '81—give or take (excuse him here) a kiss. Whew! At the time of the momentous discovery, his wife, a former schoolteacher and kind descriptive soul she is, began addressing him, "Bwana Masharubu." That, in African Swahili, the lingua franca of East Africa, perhaps the most colorfully expressive language of the world, means, "Mr. Moustache."

In a sort of good-natured, romantic, retaliatory action, with a sprinkling of jealousy for her acute command of the world's tongues, he would always leave the house after touching her cheek with his lips (notice he avoided "kiss" here?) saying something such as, "I go kuota moto mzuri ndito," which, when translated from Swahili, means "I'm going to dream by the fire, beautiful, young girl." In this case, camp or hunter's fire. This loving approach was, of course, a sort of diversionary measure or, call it hunter's psychology—or flattery—both of which are vital to Man's arsenal. . .

Time after countless time, he'd return home with his wild bounty, oft referred to as "trophies," and she, with hers. His was always of the fin, fur or feather variety in the raw, while hers were of a more finished, sophisticated leather, already tanned or bleached and shaped neatly into a pocketbook or footwear.

He took his bounty with one of the numerous weapons. She took hers with a single "weapon," notorious for its effectiveness, both long and short range. Not to mention simple, with regard to its construction and function.

This "weapon" of hers was simply a small, rectangular-shaped piece of plastic with his name and number in pimply, raised figures. It did, especially to his eyes, look formidable. And indeed, was a menacing object in the hands of anyone with her ability. Not once did she have to sight it in, tinker with it morning, noon and night, save wiping the smudge of her thumb print from its Gold Card lettering, or load it, adjust it, clean it, or, much to his dismay, **aim** the vicious little thing! The clerks statewide did that **for** her and it never failed to find the 10-ring, or bulls-eyes which, of course, was inside of one of those ugly machines with the sliding top. Yes indeed, her "weapon" was right on, right out of the envelope, and could be counted (no pun!) on to hit its target year in, year out. And he, the exemplary, poverty-stricken outdoor writer hoped with great fervor the rifling would soon wear out. The rifling in this case being those pimple-like letters and numbers upraised on said "weaponry." Eventually, of course, they did, but right behind this, in the mail and just in time was another one for her "season." Her season being endless, timeless, limitless and free – free to her!

Often he would wonder why there wasn't a waiting period, ala the controversial Brady Bill, for possession of one of those things as there was on handgun purchases? In fact, he wondered so long and hard about this, he was inspired to write to his Congressman and State Representative about it, suggesting adamantly, and with aggressive assertiveness, they propose some sort of **stiff** legislation on at least the state level, regarding the highly carefree distribution of credit cards. . .

Both the congressman and state rep wrote back, responding in a timely manner but, what was strange about the letters is, besides the contents being absolutely identical, they each appeared to be photocopies?

Nonetheless, they stated: "Dear Mr. Parry: I, too, am a hunter. I intimately and clearly understand your just concerns and sentiments. I thank you for writing me with your perceptive suggestion, but I cannot help you." Then a signature and that was it! "Boom!" as football announcer John Madden would say, "End of letter."

So their relationship continued in a business-as-usual manner, he'd hunt yonder woods and she'd hunt (more successfully!) the malls of several counties!!!

One week he tried fashioning her a hat from a coonskin but it resulted in something grossly reminiscent of a roadkill of the worst kind. So, he attempted to make up for this inadequacy as a "fashion designer" by fabricating a purse for her from an old deerhide. Her reaction to this rather attractive creation went something like this: "It's nice, Bwana, but isn't it a little big? What did you do, use the entire deer?"

Redfaced, he replied, "Yes. As a matter of fact, but taking into account your shopping extravaganzas, I still felt it may be a bit small!"

His wife, hung up considerably on the fact she had a Master's Degree in education, and forever feeling she was more erudite than he, said, wearing her familiar smirk, "Why, Bwana! Why don't we just save it for summer and use it as a tent when we go camping?"

It wasn't long until he felt a heart to heart talk with her would be in order. During that compassionate effort, he mentioned something to the effect that their pursuits were taking them their **separate** ways and, in a sense, dissolving their companionship, indeed, relationship! And she, Master of the Tongues of the World, said, "Perhaps a little, Bwana, but fear not. Our love has a yoshi moto."

Puzzled, he exclaimed, "Yoshi moto! That's not Swahili!" And certainly it was not, it was Japanese! After she'd said that, she left him standing bewildered and kissed his cheek while, at the same time, waving the little, rectangular plastic card in his face then, left for the coverts of the mall. He went to his Japanese/English dictionary expecting to find a translation of the snide type and discovered yoshi moto translated to "good foundation". He smiled to himself.

This guy he referred to as Bill Collector became too persistent with his Hey-You're-Day-Late phone calls which set him to wondering and scheming—again. He pondered the idea of convincing the Gold Card administrative folks to lower his credit limit to say, twenty-five, thirty bucks. But the lady at the east coast headquarters said, "Sir! The card alone is worth more than that!" So, no luck there. What could he do? All he wanted was to enhance their melting relationship and bring the max of the credit card down to some figure with two digits preceding the decimal point.

One late afternoon while on a lonely deer stand with little happening, he thought up a plan. Devious? Perhaps, but seemingly sound, at least at this point. . .

His rather laconic approach to the upcoming strategy went something like this after his venison-less day in Yonder Wood: "Hi Honey, I'm home! Wherefore art thou, Sweet Pea? Bwana dear is home from Yonder Forest!" His wife came down from upstairs where there was a spare room used exclusively for Gold Card acquisitions; a sort of female "trophy room." In it were tons of clothing, wagonloads of leather purses, clutches, wallets, shoes and leather boots! Enough, he thought, to fully outfit the people of Bangladesh which, at last report, was in the neighborhood of some 80-million bodies! There seemed enough leather at first glance to an inexperienced eye, to make one conjure the thought of it being cause for the demise of an entire herd of some poor Texan's Longhorned steers. And wool! Enough that he had trouble keeping her supplied with moth balls! Wool from said Texan's sheep…

102

Why when he first saw all of the wool garments, he thought of a childhood nursery rhyme that went, "Baa, baa black sheep, have you any wool?" Wondering about how they may answer today, the day and age of the Gold Card, he added these words: "No sir, no sir, thanks to the plastic tool!" We're talking here of having to buy coal cars full of moth balls, and the naphthalene fumes emanating from their upstairs was enough to bring down a Stealth Bomber! Something but something serious must be done and dear Bwana's plans were put into play somewhat haphazardly, more hurried. . .

"Well," he said, "how's Bwana's little, mzuri safi ndito?" Beautiful, bright young lady. They sat to talk and he mentioned how she was ". . .more beautiful than **any** Mona Lisa."

"But Bwana, I recall hearing you say the Mona Lisa was a homely wretch?"

"That's just what I mean, Sweet Pea, if the art connoisseurs of the world think the Mona Lisa is gorgeous, they'd be awestruck with your unparalleled beauty!" Knowing he was once again scheming.

She asked, "Okay, Bwana Punda, what's up your ragged flannel sleeve this time?"

"Nuttin, honey," he said, thinking how clever that was, "I just came to the decision that you ought to become part of my numerous hunting endeavors, that's all!" And certainly, love being pretty much what it's cracked up to be, she accepted his offer to join him, after he suggested buying her her own rifle. "I felt we'd start you out with something small, something you could use for woodchucks here in Pennsylvania but, too, something that would do well on the western front should we go for elk and mulies." Then, Bwana Punda flashed back into his brain. "By the way, Sweetie, what does punda mean?" She very nonchalantly remarked that punda meant donkey in Swahili at which time he suggested, "Honey, I think I'll start you out on a .458 Winchester magnum. Nice little caliber for a fragile lady."

Since he had a .458 of his own, she suggested she try his first, did, and immediately after shooting at a target pinned to an old, wooden chair which sat in their shooting pit, she seemed to have a change of heart; not to mention a huge mouse above her right eye and the precarious fillings of two molars, lying on the bottom of said pit.

Apologizing a thousand times over, he reminded her that she'd forgotten to pull the rifle tight to her shoulder. She was in no receptive mood! "Tight to my shoulder! Just look at that pile of splinters out there that used to be a chair! Why Bwana, it looks like Crater Lake just behind it without the dadblamed water! I'll select my own all-round caliber if you wouldn't mind!"

She pored through his library studying ballistics and all aspects of same, from sectional density of various bullets, ballistic-coefficients, feet per second and foot pounds of energy figures and long range trajectories to the energy of the recoils of various calibers. Everything, literally, she could absorb over about a week's time. Her mind, sponge-like at worst, soaked in more data than any gun writer living today knows. He tested her and she answered questions he didn't know the answers to—ever! Finally, she came to a decision that made him wince, due to both the intellect surrounding it and the economic nature of it.

"I want us to buy a nice .280 Remington caliber, once referred to as the 7mm Remington Express, in single-action, and made by New England Firearms, you know H. & R. 1871 Incorporated? Well, their neat, little Handi-Rifle comes with a recoil pad, sling swivel studs, a scope base and the action is a rugged high tensile steel which has the transfer bar to prevent unplanned discharge and everything. Why, Bwana, the barrel on it looks thicker than those on most big bore rifles, too, and you know what? You can even order other barrels for it for other types of hunting. . ."

She went on for several minutes about the virtues of the rifle she chose. Hard to argue with her desire here is how ol' Bwana felt after that lengthy dissertation. Why Jim Carmichel or the great Bob Bell, gun experts extraordinaire, might say something like, "Some gal you've got there, Bwana!" And that she was. . .

The local gun shop phoned soon after her order was placed. "Your wife's SB two rifle is in, pretty nice lookin' piece, too, and I guess you know the daggone things shoot like crazy? Whose idea? You tell her t'buy it?" He admitted, reluctantly, he didn't and hung up.

"Honey, your rifle is in at the Cooper's Gun Shop in Mansfield, wanna go in to pick it up?"

They went together and while chatting with Tim, the shop's owner, she picked out a nifty 3 x 9 power scope. "You do accept the Gold Card don't you, Tim?" He did, they left, and daydreams of increased calling from Bill Collector kept him quiet on their way home. . .

Saturday morning dawned clear and windless. "Honey, wanna sight in your two-eighty today?"

She was ready, and to his pleasure, anxious to try her rifle. "Sweet Pea, remember your promise? You said if I taught you to shoot your new rifle you'd relinquish the Gold Card, right?" She simply submitted, saying "Okay," handed over The Card and proceeded to situate herself at his (now theirs!) shooting bench.

"Okay, Moran, show what to do here please." At first he thought she'd called him a moron but came to find out later, "moran" meant tribal warrior in Swahili. He was relieved, but deep down knew that either way, she'd have been right. . .

After minimal adjustments were made, the SB-2 Handi-Rifle was consistently clustering three rounds in well under an inch at their outside spread. "Here ya go, Honey, all ready! Now, you see if you can shoot a group that small. Just do as I instructed you and don't worry if your initial attempts miss altogether, okay? It'll come slowly, but it'll come."

Not having a spotting scope, to determine where her first three rounds impacted they walked toward the target. "Well, Sweet Pea, that ain't too shabby! I can see one hole from here, right above the bull and dead center! Good shooting for a newcomer!"

As they walked the 100-yards to the target, she casually mentioned some purchases she'd made from one of his mailorder catalogs prior to letting go of the sacred Gold Card.

"I bought long-johns; beautiful all-wool plaid shirts, about a half-dozen; two light-camo coveralls; a pair of insulated camo boots in pure leather; a fluorescent orange jumpsuit for deer season; six pairs of all-wool socks, and just a whole bunch of other gorgeous attire; you know, so you'll be proud of me when we go to deer camp!" And of course he didn't show it much, but he was elated with her Gold Card prowess, not to mention her ability to decipher the hunting catalogs and their mysterious, very confusing product codes.

They arrived at the target and after close examination; he found that his little hunter-to-be wife and her SB-2 Handi-Rifle worked "together" well enough to put three 139-grainers nearly into the same hole! "Gee, Bwana, it looks like a teeny-weeny three-leaf clover, huh?" It did at that and he forced himself to smile whispering under his breath, "Why me, God?"

"Nothin' more needed here, Sweet Pea, but you know I've spent considerable time (say the last 60-seconds?) thinking about this whole idea, given it a lot of serious thought. I mean you huntin' with me and all. It gets bones-chillingly cold out there! You honestly wanna go through with the idea?"

"Only if it makes you happy, Moran. Why, you know it's the only reason I went along with it in the first place. Sure, I am a little concerned about where a body goes to the little girl's room, but little else." He casually told her the woods were in fact the world's largest little girls' and boys' room.

"Tell ya what, Hon. I'll return your Gold Card, you give me your SB-two, two-eighty Remington and we'll just scratch the whole idea, okay? Geez, Sweet Pea, I can't stand the thought of your freezing out there just to please me. Deal?" He coughed with the white lie that mildly choked him.

She looked lovingly into his eyes (forewarned this was a hunter's love story! And yes, I realize how disgusting it all is!) and asked what he would do with all the clothes she'd bought. Then without allowing him time to answer, she asked, "Haven't you heard the Shakespearean poem about the Gold Card?" She was giggling and of course, he hadn't and said so. She continued, "It goes something like this, Moran. Hear yonder call from the clothing-filled mall, is it not a sound so fantastic! If one yearns to go, just trade your rifle for that rectangular piece of plastic!" And again, they looked longingly into one another's eyes. His hand grasped the graceful, little single-shot rifle, hers snatched the pimpled Gold Card like a spring-activated, automatic vise and again, soon, they would go their separate ways. . .

Bwana Punda fell head over heels in love with the tack-driving .280 and didn't seem to mind too much that most of the clothing she'd bought through his catalogs left an awful lot of skin exposed to cold, sleet, rain and snow and yes, to anyone he might run across in Yonder Wood. Nor did he seem to mind the idea of hunting alone. It was always his way. But the boots? It was them that caused the greatest, most unbearable discomfort of this entire ordeal. It was extremely difficult walking the woods, dawn til dusk with his toes curled backwards and under his feet, rather like a fist of the foot? But, he thought, such is the life of Bwana Punda. "It does mean donkey in Swahili." He felt he was that and more for giving up the Gold Card without first buying himself a nice, new pair of hunting boots about four sizes larger. Love is blind, as they say, and as the title tells, this **is** a hunter's love story of sorts. "I'll just suffer it out with these boots," he thought, and indeed with the painful knowledge, boots of this quality have the longevity of granite rocks!

Neighbors complained for some time, they could hear him yelling after days of wearing the tortuous boots. "Honey, **please** gimme the Gold Card for one measly purchase!"

And certainly, you've guessed it. She did just that. In fact her kindness got to the point soon thereafter; she resorted back to calling him, Bwana Masharubu, Mister Moustache.

That is love from a safi moyo, pure heart. The heart of the understanding wife of an All-American hunter who no longer has sore feet or curled toes and who has regained his uhuru to boot. Uhuru? Means freedom.

Had his wife not shot a very small, 3/8ths-inch group with the .280, things could have turned out very differently.

AUTHOR'S NOTE: The people's names in this story have been changed – to prevent my being murdered. The story is real, as are the events, circumstances, and general locales. And in **no way** is this intended to belittle or slander those great cowboys and people of the West.

## "One Shot, Thirty-Aught"

My pickup inched close to the deteriorating curbside in front of what could have been the Wild West's sleaziest saloon. But then, who was I to condemn, as I was there to do a little gumshoe work and attempt to extract some inside information from the natives about hunting hotspots.

Switching on the dome light, I used the rearview mirror to scramble the neatness of my hair into an arrangement that might appear a little more pedestrian. Salvaging a desiccated cigar butt from the ashtray, I stuffed it into a corner of my mouth for the effect I felt I might need once inside, then headed for the rinky-dink front door.

"Idle-Hour" was, tastelessly painted in a hideous, puke-green enamel, apparently by someone with a terrible nervous condition, or maybe they were just drunk at the time. Still, the name seemed grossly symbolic of the kind of talk usually taking place in a joint such as this one, but, I needed information. And I felt I could turn the chatter from idle to vital ….

I couldn't help but feel a little cut-rate and somewhat guilty, like a lady of the night perhaps, as I approached the front door, but I consoled myself by thinking it was just a rundown Mom-and-Pop establishment showing years of wild cowboys' wear-and-tear weekends in town. Still, I hesitated as I reached for the old, dented brass doorknob, momentarily wishing I'd had a rubber glove for either hand. I've always been one of those uncompromising disciples of the old school who takes lightly those claims filtering out of the medical world that tell "exactly" how certain diseases are transmitted—communicable or otherwise. Always but always, distrusting the validity of same....

With that in mind, I stuffed a hand into a jacket pocket and gathered the pocket lining to form into a makeshift glove. The silkish fabric totally lacked sufficient gripping properties and my hand merely slid—no, *spun*—around the slippery knob without making noticeable progress with regard to getting the latch to retract and allow my entrance. Praise here, if you will, those exercises for the hand and forearm muscles where one squeezes a little rubber ball. I'd done them most of my life, and this, I thought, was the first time they'd ever really come into play during a time of need.

Once inside, I found the smoke was murkier than swamp fog, and the balls on the pool table cracked uncommonly loud, but the talk was at just the right volume, common of the westerner.

Right away, every snuff-tucker in the joint gave me a look, indicating, as certain as death and taxes, I wasn't one of their herd. I was accustomed to that stare, however, since I really don't look like I belong anywhere in particular. I chose my seat at the bar and settled in, ordering a Mountain Dew from whom I felt had to be Mom herself. "Howdy," I said, trying clumsily to sound native, "I'll just have me a cold Dew, please."

I fired up the old stogie butt, choked several times, then adjusted my right ear to full cock in the direction of the pool table. I don't know whether it was because I coughed with every draw of the cigar, or because they **knew** I was a stranger, but each time they got the opportunity to steal a glance toward me, they did. And each time our eyes met, I'd nod and roll the stogie from one side of my mouth to the other. In my own awkward way telling them, "I'm okay, pardner, you're okay...." I found myself strangely wishing, I'd rolled around in a mound of horse manure prior to going into this place. Knowing, though, these guys knew I wasn't a mucker or a westerner.

One, my moustache was well-trimmed and didn't hang down to the breast pocket of my shirt. And two, my jeans fit well into the category "blue", and didn't cling to my lower body so tightly they appeared to be another skin layer. Three, they couldn't see between my 30-inch legs since they weren't hideously bowed; and four, there wasn't the obvious and faded, perfectly-round mark on the hip pocket of my jeans, worn there by constantly carrying a snuff tin. Five, my belt buckle weighed-in well under the 5-lb norm common to these parts; six, the buttons on my shirt were actual buttons and not those fake, pearly snaps trimmed in fake silver. And, shameful seven, my sleeves revealed no real noticeable bicep bulge or Popeye-like forearm bulk. Eight, my face was relatively smooth when compared to the wrinkled, sun-drenched skin of the high-plainsman.

Nine, my shoes, which perhaps should have been boots, didn't carry an obscene mixture of bull-patty and alfalfa shoots, not to mention that they weren't viciously pointed like so many western boots, and so, looked alien and civilized, lacking the menacing appearance of footwear that comes to a deadly point at the toes. How often I've wondered, just how do four inches of toes fit comfortably into, say, 3/8ths an inch of boot toe? Which brings me to number ten, which was by no means the last reason on my list, but is a good place to cut off with the hope I've painted a pretty clear picture. Ten being I had all my teeth, and even though this appeared to be a place with patrons who could easily change that, I fully intended to allow my mouth the joy of retaining all of them. This meant, my being but five feet, eight inches tall, I'd have to maintain an easiness about me and a very low profile.

It wasn't long until bits and pieces of conversation about mule deer and elk began drifting into my cocked ear. Celestial and musical was dialogue with words such as, "...nice-sized bull..." and "...good-sized herd up above Eagle Creek, near the old burn" and the phrase, "Jake seen a six-pointer up on Red Ridge near Holcomb Creek." All strange territory to me, and, more and more, I felt I shouldn't have entered these barroom gates without a peavey strapped to my hip or a fistful of snoose tucked between cheek and gum.

I'd already mad a half-dozen mental notes of elk-ridden locales by the time I heard some of my favorite numbers coming from the area near the dartboard. I laughed under my breath as I thought how silly it seemed for men of this size to be playing with plastic-tipped darts? "Aren't they to be trusted with the real thing?" I thought to myself. But, as I seriously pondered that for a moment, I felt strangely grateful.

There's this appealing, melodious tone to a conversation involving rifle calibers. The several men playing with the harmless darts spoke repeatedly of the .300 Weatherby, the 7mm Remington magnum and even got into talk about the thundering, .338 Winchester magnum. The talk had me smiling to myself until it dwindled down to the idle chatter and back to elk and mulies.

It almost hurt physically, not hearing a word or two about the venerable '06 my favorite big game caliber. Not even the incredible .280 –Remington, once called the 7mm-Express which is my second favorite round and perhaps the most efficient modern-day caliber. "The 7mm's are the most efficient bullets known to modern ballistic experts, what are these guys, brain dead?" I thought. Why this group no doubt spent time with the Army's artillery units, canoneers perhaps?

The Goliath of the motley crew moved in next to me, sucked something through the gaps between his teeth, then slowly turned to look me square in the peepers. "Whaddya think, Pardner?" He asked.

"About what?" I responded, squinting my eyes to let him know I wasn't intimidated.

" 'bout what caliber might be best for elk, that's what! What's your problem, you deef?"

I could see potential trouble in his bloodshot eyes, no doubt the result of the 3.2-percent beer he'd been drinking all evening? I thought to myself, "In my younger days I would have handed him his beer glass, spun him around and planted my boot right next to his wallet." This guy seemed abrasive, but at 51-years old and streetwise, I said, "I certainly believe I could kill one with a well-placed .222 bullet, but I've sense enough not to try it. Personally, I like the caliber I use for most everything in the way of big game."

He thought a moment, belched, wiped his lips with his sleeve, then asked, "You're from back east, ain't ya?"

"Yep, mountains of northern Pennsylvania, why?"

"Why? Ya prob'ly shoot one of those cute little thutty-thutties, too, right?" He looked around toward his plastic, dart-flinging cronies for laughs of approval of what he thought to be funny stuff and they obliged.

"I own one and I've killed several deer with it, but no longer use it."

"What is it you use, then?"

"A thirty-aught six for deer, and it's also what I plan to use for elk."

"Not flat-shootin' enough for these here parts, Mister. Best latch onto a three-hunerd Winny or a seven mag. Th'old Springfield just a hope for the best round after about the three-hunerd yard marker."

I said, "That, of course, is your personal opinion only. I recall clearly doing very well with my Army aught-six at the five hundred meter range. Of course, I doubt I'd be so lacking in my compassion for deer and elk that I'd even attempt a shot that far, but I'd have little reservation about taking a shot at three or four hundred yards."

"Mister," he said in a louder volume, "you hit an elk at four hunerd with an aught-six and he'll be laughin' at ya' all the way across the Eagle Caps!"

"I think you're wrong, friend," I said, turning my attention to the Mountain Dew.

Mellowing some, he asked, "Ever hunt elk, have ya'?"

"Not yet, this will be my first elk hunt out here."

"Know where you'll be headin', do ya'?"

"Not specifically, no. Perhaps I'll head to Dean's Creek up on the Black Mountain or over Sumpter way?"

Tell ya what," he said, "me an' the boys here could use another man come Saturday if'n you'd like t'hunt with someone who knows the country? I like ya, Mister and you're welcome t'hunt with our gang."

I scrutinized his crew and realized any one of them could easily pack out an elk on his broad back, then asked, "Do you gentlemen plan on getting all sauced up the night before the opener?"

He laughed, belched, sucked something through his teeth again and said, "Naw, this here'll be our last fling til the elk's hangin'."

I looked up and into his eyes, which were flanked by deep "crows-feet" wrinkles, extended my hand in friendship and agreement and said, "Then gratefully, I accept your kind offer."

Folks around here call me Bunyon cuzza m'size, what's your name?"

"Joe," I said. "Joe Parry."

"Well Joe, tell ya what. You lay off'n that there Dew til Saturday mornin' and by golly you can go along with me'n the boys here." Then he laughed very loudly and added, "We'll be needin' another gun for the short shots!" I could feel my ears heating from embarrassment as the five of them laughed in unison. Even Mom, the saloon owner joined in, making it worse…

"Bunyon," I said, "I'd be happy with any shot at a bull as long as it's a clean one, regardless of range."

"Well, ya should get that, Pardner. Y'all be at the Truck Corral restaurant on Campbell Street at five in the mornin', come Saturday, alright?"

114

"I know the place, Bunyon, I saw it as I got off I-eighty-four when I came into town. I'll be there bright and early, and thanks for the invite."

"Well, your welcome. Bein' a Pennsylvania boy n'all, you'll be needin' all the help we can give ya. Them elk ain't a'tall like your pesky whitetails. They's big, tough, smart, nervous and mighty long winded. Why spook 'em qnd they'll run mebbe two mowl before they stop t'look back. But don't ya worry none, ya just be at the Corral Truck stop an' me an' the boys here'll show ya how ta get 'er done."

Back at the motel room, I sat scraping off little specks of snuff that had dried and stuck to my eyeglasses. Bunyon's way of talking was a bit messy and I laughed to myself as I remembered blinking every time he used a word with the letter "P" in it; like Pardner and Pennsylvania. And when he hit the word "pesky," about half of that which he had tucked smashed onto my lenses almost blinding me. But old Bunyon, he seemed decent enough as I got to understand him more, and I fell asleep thinking of elk and their being noisy, tough and smarter than pesky whitetails. Taking a last, sleepy-eyed glance at my old '06 leaning in the corner, I smiled and was gone...

Friday morning found me walking the streets of Baker in a lonely, bored mood. An old timer pulling a wagonload of aluminum cans advised me as to where to go when I asked him where there might be a rifle range. I felt I should check out the '06, AKA, the peashooter.

"Ya just head out t'Virtue Flats, take the two-tracker jus at t'bottom of the hill on the Richland road, where it leads up t'bottom of the hill on the Richland road, where it leads up t'th Interpretive Center on the ol' Oregon Trail. It's th' last turnoff out the straight-away b'for ya head uphill. Out 'thair ya'l see lottsa brass and targets layin' aroun'. That'll be it."

I found the place okay and pinned a target on a box at a stretched 100-yards. Across the pickup hood, the first round centered perfectly and just about 2 ½ inches high. "Perfect," I said aloud. Then I picked up a few empty snuff tins and set them up at about fifty yards—and proceeded to drill the center of each one. "No work needed here," I said, and still bored I jumped into the pickup and headed toward town, dodging jackrabbits all along the two-tracker."

I was at the Truck Corral early and the Bunyon crew pulled in right on time. As Bunyon walked up to the pickup, I rolled down the window and immediately removed my eyeglasses. Just in time as it turned out, for Bunyon blurted out, "Mornin' there Partner!" A great emphasis on the "P."

"Y'all ready to kill ya'self an elk there, Pennsylvania?"

Bunyon rode with me and we followed the rest of the crew who were riding in Slim's rig. After we left the paved road, we'd traveled about 30-minutes when Bunyon said, "Be at th' Five Corners here pretty quick."

We were just at the threshold of the vast Eagle Caps and I began feeling a bit apprehensive. "Awful danged quiet aint'cha Joe? Nervous are ya?"

"Not really, Bunyon. Just thinking about how small a man feels out here compared to home."

"She's some kinda big country, alright. Why she'll eat a man up and mebbe never spit 'im out! But don't ya be worryin' none, me an' the boys'll keep an eye on ya." He laughed and said, "Why we just might even get ya a close shot for that peashooter of yourn!" Enter considerable laughter here...Bunyon's!

We pulled off to the side of the road behind Slim's lead. Bunyon announced, and I ducked just in the nick of time "This is it Pennsylvania!" Slim and Bunyon laid out the hunt plans. I was to work a sidehill along what they referred to as Red Ridge, and walk it until I reached the road below where we'd parked "the rigs."

About a third of the way into the hunt, I heard the unmistakable sound of branches being broken. "No wind," I thought as I looked into the treetops. I kept walking. Slowly, I pussyfooted my way along through the misty rain. The day was genuinely miserable, the red clay, sloppy and difficult to navigate. I was above the clouds, or what looked similar to clouds, but could have been just been puffy layers of thick fog? The air was still which was good for never did wind aid the hunter's cause—especially, mine. Hearing another loud "crack!" in the distance, I again looked to the treetops for signs of wind. None! Then "crack!" again. I immediately remembered Bunyon's final words to me: Elk'r noisy turds…" That's when it hit me.

"Elk!" I thought aloud. I then scoured the adjacent sidehill across the canyon, then the ridgetop above. That's when they appeared as giants, ghosting from the thicket of pines. There appeared to be a dozen or more in this herd, but I didn't know. In seconds, I put all my hunting prowess into play, slid down the side hill a little and got onto a flat rock to sit for my shot should there be one. I settled my elbows between my knees, military style, and cranked the variable scope up to what I later learned was the 6x position. Taking another look, this time through the scope, I could see the lead cow staring back at me.

Through the scope, we seemed to be looking eyeballs to eyeballs. "She sees me!" I thought. Quickly I determined the range to be near four-hundred yards, give or take? Just then a bull, heavily racked, antlers jerking with every bite he took of whatever it was he was grazing, stepped into the clearing. I settled the horizontal crosshair to show perhaps two-inches of daylight between his withers and the wire, then touched the trigger.

He dipped in the front and simultaneously wheeled around to his right and disappeared so quickly there was simply no time for a follow-up shot. "Son of a gun!" I said aloud, not knowing for certain whether I'd hit him. Everything however, felt and looked good as far as the bull taking a hit. I thought at the time, I was just so accustomed to deer dropping dead in their tracks and this elk didn't do that?

Moments later, "Hey there, Pennsylvania, who was shootin'?" It was, of course, Bunyon.

I had my story told before he got to me. "Think ya hit 'im, do ya?"

Not wanting to sound too eastern, I said, "Yep, I'd say so. Let's go over there for a looksee, huh?"

"Only shot the one time, did ya?" Bunyon queried.

"Yep. All I had time for. Besides, I've never had to shoot twice with this aught-six. But that big bull? I'm not real sure…"

"C'mon Pardner," Bunyon said, "let's head on over there t'see if ya hit 'im at least."

It took nearly twenty-five minutes for us to navigate the hillside down, then the draw and the other, steep side hill. It was tough going and of course, Bunyon got there first. He yelled, "By juniper, ya hit 'im alright, looky here." Bunyon pointed to a tuft of cut hair and a spot of blood about the size of a quarter which was the only visible evidence of a hit. I looked over Bunyon's shoulder and beyond about 30 yards and spotted my bull about three elk strides away. He was piled up near some mahogany and appeared stone dead.

"There he lays, Bunyon!" I pointed, Bunyon turned to look.

"Well I'll be dogged!" He said, "Why that's a good four hunerd crossed that draw. Ya done good, Pennsylvania!" I was unable to avoid the wet snoose spray that time; too tired…

The bull took the 165-grain bullet through both lungs and it never exited. All the shock spent killing him instantly. I stroked the thick, straw-colored coat of the massive bull, awestruck with its size. I gave thanks in my heart and at the moment felt the oldest remorseful feeling known to man, his glazed eye staring back at me created a moment of respectful silence and I wondered again as I had countless times: "Will I ever feel any better about an animal dying?" I wouldn't. I knew it…

The other members of the Bunyon crew were nearly up the side hill when Bunyon called out, "Old flatlander Pennsylvanian here got 'im a bull from clean crossed that there canyon with his peashooter!"

I patted Bunyon's shoulder and curtly remarked, "Like I told ya, Bunyon, one shot, thirty aught!"

The crew in chorus, laughed, and Bunyon squeezed my shoulder saying, "Lucky is all, just plumb lucky!" I was lucky my glasses caught no spray when he said "plumb" with considerable lip action on the "P."

We stood there admiring the elk as Bunyon removed the ivory teeth from its mouth. Feeling pretty good by then, I thought I'd have some fun with him and the crew. "You know, of course, Bunyon, that the shot had little to do with luck? I know that old aught six better than I know my wife. Tell ya what, I'll prove how well she shoots and just how well I know 'er, how about that?"

He looked up at me with questioning eyes and said, "How?"

"Just Watch," I said, pulling a snuff tin from my jacket pocket. I allowed just its sides be seen, then unshouldered my Ruger. Holding the snuff can, I said, "You see this here snuff can, Bunyon? Well, I'm gonna toss it into the air and put a hole through its middle with old one shot here."

He looked over at his crew and said with widened eyes, "Ta hell ya are!"

"You just watch, cowboy." I said.

"Oh I'ma watchin', Pennsylvania, I'ma watchin'. You hit that there snooze can and me an' the' boys here'll drag out this here bull for ya! Won't we boys?" They all nodded agreeably...

Slim, the quiet one of the bunch added, "You hit that tin and we'll drag your bull all the way to Pennsylvania, Joe!"

I reached down and gathered some small stones to place in the can for throwing weight, then sent it sailing high and toward the down slope of the hill. The '06 barked while still just above my hip. Bunyon ran to get the can just a second after it had hit the ground then returned wearing the look of a little boy who'd just seen a ghost. "Be damned if'n it ain't got a hole plumb through the middle, boys!" He held it out for everyone to see, rubbing his summer-sausage sized thumb over the hole, almost affectionately...

119

"Like I told ya, Bunyon – one shot, thirty aught!"

I saw no need to tell them the snuff tin was one I'd shot a hole through on Virtue Flats Friday morning. I felt ignorance is bliss and I wanted them to remain happy, for indeed they were a good bunch of boys. There was little need to tell them the real story and I felt it would provide them with story-telling material in future bull sessions at the Idle Hour. Too, I felt it would give reason to respect the '06 and Pennsylvanians; perhaps all easterners?

The long trip home was peaceful. I was happy with my first bull elk but felt a sense of loss as I strangely missed peering through snuff-speckled eyeglasses. Missing it more than just a little…

I laughed until my eyes teared as I thought about the bet old Bunyon had made regarding packing my bull off that mountain. But, tough as it was, they did it in good humor and short order. A good lot they were…

Bunyon and I exchanged addresses so we might keep in touch and again, hunt together. About a week or so after I'd been home, I received a small package in the mail. It was from old Bunyon.

Inside was a note and a snuff tin with an '06 hole punched through its center. The note read: "…this here snooze tin fell outta yer pocket when ya bent t'put the rocks in the one ya had in yer hand that day on the mountain. I figured t'let you have yer fun with m'boys but when ya gits back aroun' these parts, I'll be expectin' ya to buy me a Mountain Dew…" Of course, this isn't the manner in which the letter was written but rather, how I interpret it. And sure, I'll buy him a case of Dew, but I'm going to be doing some teasing once I return.

You see, he signed his letter, "Your Cowboy Buddy, Bunyon." I can barely wait to tell him how "corny" his letter was…

AUTHOR'S NOTE: Bill was one of the most naturally funny men I've ever known and it always seemed to me that the more serious he tried to become, the funnier he was. Not an easy man to sit next to while eating, let alone hunting. He was, in appearance, reminiscent of Curly of Three Stooges fame; the original Curly.

No friend since or before him did for my spirits what Bill did unintentionally and so often....As long as I live, I'll not forget this hunt, the tremendous quantity of hunter orange or the smell of eucalyptus that, I'd bet, permanently permeated the bark of every tree in the woods where Big Bill hunted. If eucalyptus has any preservation quality, Bill is probably in better shape now than the great mummies, such as King Tut. And yes, Bill would approve of this statement and laugh about it. He loved to laugh, loved to make others laugh regardless of the price he'd have to pay. To this day, I think Big Bill bought the hunter orange mentioned in the story here, just to bring happiness to my heart. And it did. In fact, it still does, bless his departed soul...

## "Roadkills and White-Lies"

A steel gray, November sky bullied away the low-slung Indian summer sun while the last of autumn's tenacious leaves finally succumbed to aggressive winds out of the northwest.

Familiar smells, musky in nature from decaying forest leaves and ground duff filled the air with the certainty that Nature was making Her perennial announcement: "Buck season rides a hurried wind . . ." And this signaled a time for sacred indulgence for the infamous, two-man rank and file of the Bullseye Bunch, Infallible.

And rest easy: these two are not greed-stricken, poor shooting, loathsome, litter-tossing, disrespectful to Nature men; these men of the B.B.I.. They'd spent weeks in preparation getting things just right – clothing, rifles, and hickory-smoked jerky for quick, woodland snacks. These men well respected the quarry of the season upcoming, the whitetailed deer, and each harbored a deep-set love for all wild things, and wild places and nurtured that fondness on a continuing and highly relentless basis. In this sense, then, and perhaps only this aspect of their lives, were they in fact, infallible....

Little Joe's phone rings early Sunday morning: "Has to be Big Bill, again!" Joe said as he stumbled to the phone. This, according to accurate records written upon a scratch pad near the phone, was the ninetieth call from Big Bill in his child-like excitement over the buck season upcoming. Calls that came at all hours of the day and night and for all reasons, mostly unimportant insofar as substance! But, that was Bill, the giant pussycat in the huge body of a man; little things meant a lot to his big, Teddy Bear heart and childish mind. And, as abstract and bewildering as it seemed to Joe, Joe loved his buddy regardless . . .

"Hello, hello, hello, Short Shooter! Is your sleepy, burned-out mind aware of what Sunday it is?"

"Yeah, yeah, Porky, I know what Sunday it is! Pick me up in thirty minutes and don't forget your rifle, shells, targets and a big thermos of cinnamon tea, the tea being for your illustrious leader! And also, Fat Boy, if you're driving don't forget your vehicle!"

"How could I forget my Ram, little buddy, and what's this tea business?" Bill questioned.

"Yes, whacky Willy, tea! It'll be easier on the nerves than that 10W, 40-weight coffee we usually drink and enable us to hold steadier on the sand bags. Bye! See ya in thirty!"

The initial shots from Big Bill's .32 lever fell nearly a foot low and another half-foot right. "Good grief, waddling Willy, it's no wonder you never got a deer what with the way this saddle gun is shootin'! You are fortunate to have befriended the master of the Bullseye Bunch. Just watch what a few expert adjustments and an eagle eye will do." In short order, Bill's venerable old, thirty-two Winchester clustered three rounds tightly and centered just about 2-inches above the bull. "There ya go, Billy me deer slayer. Why, you could cover that group with a nickel."

So, the two were pretty much ready. Joe literally pounded the last minute hunt instructions into Bill's resilient mind. "And don't you dare bring a single eucalyptus cough drop with you tomorrow. Not in your pocket, anywhere! Bill, can you even imagine what those awful things smell like to a deer?" Bill was rather addicted to these aromatic lozenges and always carried a good supply in just about every pocket.

"No cough drops, Little Buddy, I promise!"

"And," Joe added, "no aftershaves, stinky hair tonic, no flowery smelling anti-perspirants and please, none of that terrible watermelon bubble gum you're forever gnawing at!"

"Nuttin' stinky Joe, I promise. Nuttin' stinky. I promise!"

"Okay," Joe said, "now get your flabby derriere home and be at my door by five a.m. in the mornin'. Got it?"

"Got it, Little Buddy, got it. But what if I come around a little early?"

"Don't!" Joe said, looking sternly into Bill's little-boy sky blue eyes, "Just please, don't!"

Bill's knock on Joe's door the following morning, must certainly have registered in the low fives on the Richter scale! And yes, it was 3:45 a.m.! "Bill, for cryin' out loud, I just went to sleep a few hours ago! I thought I told you. . ."

"I know, Little Buddy, I know! I was up and about and all set to do as you asked this mornin' when I discovered I was outta dental floss. And ol' Billy here can't do nuttin' before he flosses. Got any floss, partner?"

"Shut up and get in here before you awaken the neighbors! Geezooey, Bill, you're like a dadblamed kid!" Joe went and turned on the radio for weather information as Bill, heavy-footed, stepped into the kitchen.

As Joe fumbled with the radio, Big Bill paced about the kitchen. "Shhh! Geez, Bill, you sound like a rhino walkin' on a hollow log. You're gonna wake everyone!" Joe switched on the kitchen light, turned to look at Big Bill and was immediately blinded! "Holy mackerel, Billy! That's more fluorescent orange than I've **ever** seen in one place! Good grief, man, you look like the Orange Bowl with feet!"

"Looks pretty doggone nice, heh Partner? Whaddya say?"

"Yeah, Bill, **real** nice. Looks real nice. Factory most likely shut down after making that outfit, no doubt outta dye! Why I never realized there was that much hunter orange in the county, fer cryin' out loud! Now, go into the powder room there and get your floss." Moments later Bill emerged from the powder room. The radio weather report called for "increasing cloudiness with high winds expected until early evening." Bill's hollow-sounding snow-pak boots echoed throughout the kitchen. Walking up to Joe, he whispered, "Can't go nowheres, 'specially huntin' before my flossin', Little Buddy."

Joe looked up at Bill and saw he had a horrendous amount of dental floss which had the distinct likeness of a rather large bird's nest, save the trailing strand that Bill directed between his pearly whites. "What in blazes you doin', Bill? Goin' bass fishin' or deer hunting? Why there's enough floss there to fill the spool on a deep sea fishing reel!"

Poor Big Bill. He stood there like a kid, embarrassed to the point where his eyes watered profusely. "Yeah, I know Little Buddy. I couldn't get that there little blade on the container to cut 'er off and it just kept comin' and comin' and comin'. This here's the whole roll! I owe ya one partner, sorry."

"Just drink your coffee Bill, and let's get rollin', okay?"

Bill began to laugh and having difficulty getting out what he thought was joke of the year! "Hey, Short Stop, how's about we take along this here floss and drag out our deer with it?"

Joe just shook his head left to right and smiled sincerely at Big Bill's unique, lovable way, then said, "Billy me lad, you get your deer today, old Rank here will personally carry it out on his shoulder! Now. Let's go!"

Bill followed Joe to Mr. G's farm. Joe had a story to cover at the deer check station and Bill mentioned that he may want to hunt past noon, which was when Joe planned to leave the woods, deer or no. The weather promised a miserable first day, too, and Joe was worried about Big Bill's success, wanting him to get his buck in the worst way. "You just hunt if I decide to go, Bill. No sense both of us cutting our first day short. . ."

They parted at the vehicles and went to their respective stands, the better of the two being "given" to Big Bill. "Good luck, Little Buddy!" Bill whispered.

"And the very best of luck to you, Big Boy. Put one down and out in my honor, will ya?"

"Try," Bill whispered back, "I'll sure try. Thanks!"

Joe thought about Bill all the while he pussyfooted to his stand, thinking, "It would be the most wonderful thing in God's world if that big-hearted teddy bear got his buck and by golly the big lug deserves to feel the thrill of that at least."

The winds of promise blew savagely. Decaying trees were uprooted and fell viciously to the ground, while large limbs snapped and were tossed onto the ground all around Joe's stand. Clouds raced by in the threatening sky and the morning hunt was fast losing its flavor. Joe thought, "I'd best go after Bill and call it a day. Nothing will be moving in this weather but the trees. . ." However, even before Joe got himself together to leave, he saw a blinding mass of fluorescent orange walking toward him.

"Howdy there Little Windbucker! Think we ought to pack 'er in?"

"Yeah," Joe said disgustedly, "let's just head for the Palace and hope for a better tomorrow." Joe at that moment, was able to easily detect the strong aroma of eucalyptus over-powering the muskiness of the forest, which in itself was powerful on this damp morning. "Cough drops, Bill?"

"Yeah. I know, I know. I promised Joe, but that daggone wind had me a nervous wreck. I just knew it was blowin' away our day and it'd turn out to be a total loss, so when I found a few cough drops I had stashed away in that old oak tree hole, I couldn't resist. But at least I waited til the wind was so strong I kinda knew you'd call off the hunt. Not mad at ol' Billy, are ya?"

Bill's look made Joe spare him a good tongue lashing, and off they headed toward their vehicles. Big Bill's Ram headed out first.

As Joe came down Mr. G's red dog drive, he could see up onto a mountain directly in front of him. Several hunters were lining up to drive out a big section of woods. "By golly," he thought, "they may just push one outta there!" So, instead of turning left toward town, Joe went right then parked his truck at the first wide spot on the dirt road. He climbed part way up the mountain to the open field where the hunters had lined up for their drive, then situated himself in a good vantage point where he could see anything that may slip back through the hunters. It was strangely flat there, a bench of sorts on the smallish hillside.

He'd no sooner caught his breath when he heard shots. One, then two more. Several moments of silence followed and Joe's eyes were watering from the wind blowing into his eyes and the strain of staring into the woods' edge. Just as he was about to call his plan a futile effort, two deer burst from the woods—unaware he was there—and raced across the opening. On one knee, Joe followed them through his scope. "Tough shot, quartering away. . ." His mind raced, the bucks turned giving him less "away" angle and he touched off a round at the deer on the near side, fortunately, the larger of the two. The rest is history. Old "One Shot, Thirty-Aught" had done his job again.

126

Field work done, liver and heart in a plastic bag and secured in his jacket, Joe headed downhill toward the pickup. "Easiest draggin' I ever done. . ."

As Joe pulled into the Palace parking lot he saw Big Bill pacing like a huge, orange mother hen just inside the big window in the front of the restaurant. Bill ran outside to greet him, hollering even before he was all the way out the door. "Where in tarnation you been, Joe? Why I was worried sick! Been here well over an hour and was just about t'come after your hide. What happened, I was so worried I could hardly eat!"

Bill's sincerity was evident in his puppy-dog blue eyes and he reached over and gave Joe a bear hug, shaking him with the affection of a partner who **really** cared about his well being. Then, Big Bill spotted the big eight-point buck in the back of Joe's truck.

Joe saw the shock in Bill's eyes, and at the same time, the hurtful look. Joe's mind raced again, for he wouldn't hurt Bill for the world and all its big bucks.

"What is that, Little Buddy?" Bill asked. "Ya mean t'tell me you got ya a buck after I left you?" Bill's face was bland, drained of all its color, and Joe knew it hurt Bill seeing that buck, knowing of course how badly Bill had wanted one. Joe felt one Lily White Lie wouldn't make his Maker angry?

"Naw, Billy. That there's a roadkill I picked up on my way in. Some hunter musta wounded him up in the woods and he got hit when he was crossin' the road? I phoned old Warden Regis from the filling station and he said to bring it on in if I wouldn't mind. Gonna take it to the orphanage, I'd guess?"

Wide-eyed, Bill rubbed the thick brow tine on the antler. "Boy, Joe, he's a dandy ain't he? Wish we could've seen him out there this morning, huh?" Not giving Joe an opening to answer, he went on. "Ya know, Partner, I wouldn't have cared who got him, me or you! Golly, he's beautiful, ain't he?"

127

Joe left, broken-hearted at best, and told Bill he'd best get the buck to Warden Regis. "Howdy Rege, how's about giving this buck to the orphanage for me?" The warden thanked him and he left for home, feeling rather certain he'd done the right thing, proper in that it would spare his buddy Big Bill any hurt? But somewhat saddened himself, thinking he may not have his cherished winter venison. . .

Their buck season, even though Joe's secretly ended earlier, went without incident. Joe accompanied Bill just to share the usual joys that seemed to forever follow this pair known as, the Bullseye Bunch. Bill went without his first buck even with Joe helping and driving out different areas. Joe's buck filled the stomachs of precious orphans. . .

"Well, Billy, Monday is the start of antlerless season and neither of us have winter venison. Ya gonna score Big Boy or ain't ya?" Bill shrugged his shoulders and worked that smile onto his face that completely dimpled his rosy cheeks.

"Well, by jiminy, Joe," he said, "I'm a ready as a Freddy. I'm just hopin' things go better than they did for our two weeks of buck season! You?"

"While we are on the glorious but unproductive subject of buck season, Billy me boy, do you, the second highest ranking official of the B.B.I., recall telling your leader of same, that you were so worried about my tardiness opening day, that is when I arrived late at the Palace, you could **hardly eat**? I then, would like to share with you, you blue-eyed blimp, this list I compiled consisting of the things Rosie the waitress told me you ate in the hour or so you awaited my arrival." The list was obnoxiously lengthy: At least one and one-half pots of coffee, four uncommonly large slices of tooth-rottening pie of various types, a large bowl of music-making chili con carne, three foot-long chili dogs, several dozen saltines complete with whipped butter for combating indigestion, two large glasses of strawberry milkshake topped with whipped cream and maraschino cherries, a softball-sized blueberry muffin and a handful of after-dinner mints. Joe then held the list to Bill's bulbous nose. Bill's face reddened and carried that familiar, childish look of guilt, much like a cat who'd just devoured his master's blue-ribbon goldfish.

Bill squealed, "I was worried, Joe! Truly, truly, I was. I told you that, yes. But I **never** said I wasn't hungry, just that I could **hardly** eat!" Joe patted Bill's mammoth shoulder to help him through this moment of emotional stress.

"Bill," he said, "was that hardly eat, or heartily eat? Your in-shape, well-muscled leader here doesn't eat that much in a week's time!"

The doe opener found the two B.B.I boys together in the darkness on the ridge above McGinnis Hollow. They drank tea at the vehicle, whispering their plans for the day back and forth, then parted company with the customary, "Good lucks." Joe, tough as he's not, whispered silent prayers for Big Bill's success all the way to his morning stand. "I love that big poop, by golly, and I sure hope he scores this mornin'."

Joe, on stand, "Ten o'clock and nothing? Guess I'd better do some pushing for ol' Bill." He got up and walked toward Bill's stand, some distance away and within say, 100 yards, he could detect the heavy (very heavy!) odor of cough drops, eucalyptus no less, and when he got to Bill, he discovered Bill's cough drop addiction to be at an all-time high!

"I though I told ya no cough drops, Sneaky Pete?" Bill's stand area was completely surrounded by strewn wrappers, which certainly he always burned prior to leaving. But Joe was hot under the collar and stared sternly into Bill's glazed eyes.

"Didn't have a one Little Sherlock! Not one! So there, put that into your pipe and puff it!"

"Then Billy, how do you account for all these wrappers I just waded through?"

"Just watch this!" Big Bill unwrapped another cough drop, telling Joe to sit and be still a moment. He then tossed it to the base of a hickory den tree about 15-yards away. A large gray squirrel appeared from inside the tree, apparently watching them all along, picked up the cough drop, then scampered right back into its den. "See there, Little Buddy, told ya!" Bill said, "Been feeding that little nut buster these things all morning. Dunno what in tarnation he's doin' with 'em, but he grabs and runs every time I toss one out there!"

"Yeah, yeah, Bill. And you're all the while hoping your next squirrel fricassee tastes like eucalyptus, right?"

Bill began elaborating loudly on what a fine idea that might be when Joe cut him short. "C'mon, let's go get us some venison."

"Bill, I'm gonna push out the hollow down there." Joe pointed, adding, "You stay right here and don't move a layer of blubber until I come after you, understand? And good luck!"

Not long after Joe began his push, he heard the sounds of deer moving way out ahead, then seconds later, bang! Then bang, again. And two more bangs! Joe wondered, "What in the world is that gorilla doing? That little thirty-two of his is right on the money?"

After Joe got to within ear-shot of Big Bill, he could see the giant of a man pacing back and forth like an expectant father and soon was able to see that Big Bill was standing over one fat doe of the season! Joe was ecstatic, running the last 35 or 40-yards.

"Billy, me deer slayer of the chubbiest kind, ya got one! Your first deer, Billy, way to go!" Joe all but broke Big Bill's back, slapping it over and over, but rest easy, Bill couldn't feel a mortar hitting his back what with all the blubbery layer beneath his clothing. The joy was shared, and Bill stood there smiling ear to ear, unable (a rare moment!) to speak as Joe scrutinized the deer walking around it over and over and over. Joe's heart was as full as it had ever been which was proof of the love he had for his partner.

"Why did ya have t'shoot four times, Billy?"

"Well, Little Buddy, she was over the gully there, just lyin' up in the laurel and I didn't want to shoot her lyin' down so I shot three times b'fore I could get her t'movin'. By jiminy, Joe, if I'm gonna be a deer hunter, I'm gonna be a fair one always!" Joe thought, what a heart this big bear of a man had, deepening his respect for Bill.

Joe dragged Bill's plump, corn-fed deer for nearly an hour toward the truck. "'preciate your draggin' her out for me, Joe, I'm whupped!"

"Billy, I promised you I'd carry her out on my shoulders if ya got one, didn't I?"

"Yep, ya did at that, Joseph!"

"One thing about your leader, Billy, is he never tells a lie. Especially to a fellow member of the B.B.I."

"Izzat right, Shorty and teller of the lily-white lie?"

"That is keeerect, m'friend, keeeeeeerect!" Joe said.

"Then how come," Bill questioned, "old Warden Regis found a neat little thirty-caliber hole in the neck of that eight-pointer you told me was a roadkill back in buck season?

"Was a roadkill, Billy!"

"Was not, ya short fibber!"

"Was, Billy. It was!"

"Joe!" Big Bill's blue eyes watered, begging for the truth.

"Well, okay," Joe said, head down shamefully, "but if a guy looks real hard up there on the bench where I shot it, there **are** faint, ancient tracks where there used to be a loggin' road!"

"Ya know what?" Bill said, his heart melting, "If you wasn't so dadblamed short and fragile, I'd love ya t'death with one a'my famous bear hugs! That was the biggest buck you ever shot, Joe and I knew then why ya did what ya did, least I thought so. That's why I questioned old Regis. Still, I sorta thought when ya left the diner that day, ya'd take that ol' buck home and hide 'im in the deep freeze."

"Billy me lad, that buck would have put the coupe de grace on my old heart had I eaten a single tenderloin off him. Remember, William, in this B.B.I. organization, the other

131

guy always comes first and your leader merely did what his heart dictated. . ."

Doe season ended and Joe hadn't gotten one since all his opportunities were too chancy. After his first day back at the Observer newspaper, he came home tired and in a dismal mood, common to the deer hunter when seasons end.

He walked into the kitchen and upon the table lay a note, reading: "Hi, Joe! There are two tender Porterhouse steaks in the frig for you and the wife for supper. And if you'll look in the deep freeze, you'll find your kindly wife allowed me to stock you with a grand side of grain-fed beef. Anyone who would give away a whole venison, the biggest buck of his dumb life, deserves to suffer through beef **all** winter!" Of course this letter was written with proper spelling and grammar for the sake of the readers' understanding and it was signed, "Your Best Pal, Big Bill The Deerslayer."

There was a post-script which said: "Under all that tender beef is exactly one-half of my deer. Your share of the winter venison ya big dope! Eat it in good health cause next year I ain't givin' you a single pound of my deer! But then again, I just might. Especially if I stumble upon some old road kill on Mr. Georgetti's farm with a thirty-two caliber hole in it! Bye! Billy!"

Ya just gotta love this guy, don't you?

EPILOGUE: I'd moved my family to Oregon to do some Western hunt writings after the doe hunt with Big Bill.

The next buck season on Mr. Georgetti's farm, Bill went to a spot I insisted he go on opening day. "...and no cough drops! Do not leave that spot until at least 10:30 A.M. Understand?"

Bill did understand and killed the biggest buck ever off Mr. "G's" big farm. I learned during a long-distance phone call to Mr. "G."

It was, of course, Bill's first, only, and last buck. He died that following spring, as did a very significant part of his "short buddy," Joe.

AUTHOR'S NOTE: This piece was written just 16 days after my first heart attack. There were two inspirations for it: one was my desire to get a message to people who have had similar health problems. That being, don't give up on those things in life you love to do; but, at the same time, don't tackle the "mountain" too soon. . .

The story tells of a marvelous animal, our family dog, Bear. A deeper love than his for each of our family members, I've not before seen. And soon, if indeed I live long enough, I will write a story of this truly great animal that may bring revelation to the world. Bear is unbelievable. I owe him far more than just my very life and pray so I don't fall short as I try to give back all he's given unto my life; the love, the purpose, the loyalty and a great deal of the spark needed to simply keep on living. This one, Bear, my friend, is for you. And in my heart I know you'd love my sharing it with the world. . .

You **are** special, my friend. I hope you don't mind my telling of it in this piece I've dedicated to you? As human as you are most times, you'd no doubt blush if in fact you could read. You can't, can you boy?

### "An Autumn Heart"

A man thinks very deeply of many things when he thinks he is soon going to die. Mainly of those things in life he most loves; his wife, children, his dog and yes, those autumnal rituals which, of course, are hunts in his most favored woodlands of the high country. And during such times, he may pray, perhaps harder, and with more feeling, desire and need than ever before.

The prayer may go something like this: "Please God, just let me hold and love and touch my children one more time. Just one more warm kiss goodnight for them, for my wife. And how about allowing me one more rub behind the velvet-like ears of our dog and maybe God, just maybe mind you, one more taste of the autumn woods would be in order? One more deep, inhaling breath to let in the musky smell of dying forest litter? Then I'll come to wherever it is You want me. You can wait one more day or so can't You? Just let me fill up my autumn heart once more before You take me to your neck of the woods. I promise that if you'll just let me smell burnt gunpowder one more time, kiss my wife, children and dog, I'll go peacefully but, if not, I'm afraid I'm going to have to fight and win those needed moments for myself, God. And yes, Boss, I know in my heart it would be wrong to fight this thing, this thing so natural, but I am rather young. And as a father of two, a husband and my dog's best friend, I must fight, you see. Please don't think of me as ungrateful for You giving me this gift of Life for it's been ever so precious to me. I just would like one more, okay, one last helping. With your permission, of course. . ."

That wasn't quite the prayer, word for word, but it does tell some of what I ask for on October 13th, 1996, one month before my 54th birthday, when I had a severe heart attack and lay helpless and hurting like never before on an E.R. bed in a Tioga county hospital. And certainly, without having been heard and answered by a gracious God this story wouldn't be. . .

My son, Justin, had to bring my wife to town to retrieve the family wagon for I'd driven myself to the hospital. When he walked into my stall in the E.R., the look on his face was enough to bring tears to my eyes. Obviously, he was frightened and deeply concerned, not to mention at a loss for words.

Reaching for his trembling hand I said, with a half-dozen wires, tubes and needles dangling from various parts of my body, "Don't you worry, Partner, I'll be out of here before the grouse opener on Saturday." I added my warmest smile, hoping to comfort his frightened heart. He just looked at me, his pillar of strength and best friend, and his words, whatever they were, wouldn't come. He merely shook his head from side to side.

"God, I hope so, Pop. I love you, see ya later. . ." With that he walked away and didn't look back. . .wearing a look on his face I won't ever forget.

Somehow I knew I'd be all right; up and out for our first grouse hunt of the year on October 19th. But this time, wise old Pop was wrong and somehow, the wanting to just be there seemed more important than even before—in some 41 seasons.

The doc, honest and up front, which I respect in all men, said, "Mr. Parry, this is serious. There's considerable damage to your heart and I wouldn't plan on going anywhere for a while, especially hunting."

"Hey Doc, you don't know me very well. That EKG just shows another hurdle in my life and I've always been a pretty good jumper. You just do what's gotta be done and I'll provide all the fight. I'll be there opening day with Justin."

He smiled, shook his graying head and said, "I've never in my career had anyone take a heart attack quite so lightly and of all things, place hunting so high on a priority list when he's not even out of the emergency room yet."

"Doc, it isn't that hunting is so high on my list of priorities, it's the being there and what I share with my son during hunting season that's priceless. The mutual, yet unspoken feelings, the shared peace, the magic of frosty mornings in the woods together, the quiet. It's a kind of rejuvenation of the love between father and son. Like sunshine and water is to a tree or plant, it helps us grow together and understand one another more intimately. Kinda puts back and adds some to what the rest of the year may have depleted somewhat. You know? Those times we didn't quite see eye to eye? Yes indeed, Doc, there's far more to hunting with a child than guns and supplementing the old larder. Fact is, Doc, I never really knew my son until we began hunting together. Kids, for some reason, open up out there. Like flowers, I tell ya, they expose their deepest feelings, bare their souls and free up all those things that may be nagging them inside. It's the magic of autumn, Doc—and the greatest of the many benefits a father gets from hunting.

"Heck, now when I buy a license it's more of a ticket to be alone with Justin than it is a tag for a buck's ear. More often than not, we end up sitting around a small hickory limb and pine cone fire forgetting what in heck we came for and just enjoying each other's company. And even though we almost always bring home the winter venison, Doc, it's never been what's most important to us. We learn when we're out there. About nature as well as each other and because of hunting seasons, Justin and I share a relationship I consider priceless. And he, too, knows the magic of something I call the autumn heart. And one day he'll share it with his children, my grandchildren—that is if you ever get back to working on my heart and fixing it so it'll beat long enough for me to meet them."

The doc laughed while reading another EKG printout and said, "Maybe I ought to start hunting with my wife and daughter. . ."

"Can only help any relationship, Doc. Now, take two aspirins and call me in the mornin'. I'll mail you the bill." He laughed again.

October 18th I was still lying in a hospital bed and the next morning would be the early small-game opener. Time to talk with my cardiologist or, at worst, the hospital cook who had about as much culinary imagination as a paper clip. Everything I ate tasted the same and that wasn't good. In fact bland would be an over-zealous description of the food, including the milk. They said it was skim but it was so clear, I could easily have read the Game Laws through it without the aid of polarized glasses.

And I'd used enough bedpans to almost permanently drop my body temperature to well below the normal 98.6 degrees! I had enough cords, of varying types, strung from my bruised body to wire a small village and, between those and several yards of intravenous tubes they were keeping me alive with, I looked like a mound of pasta lying there. I was going nuts, had to get out and at one point didn't care about

136

my dying as long as it was in the woods and not in a hospital bed where nary a grouse could be found and the food was bound to get me sooner or later. I could envision the headlines vividly: "**Outdoor Writer Dies From Boredom and Bland Food**."

The head cardiologist finally gave in and signed my discharge order that Sunday; the day after the opening Saturday. And, with the understanding that I not hunt for at least a week to ten days and only for a real short time. ". . .about an hour at most, Mr. Parry, and only if you go but right across the road from your home as you indicated to me earlier."

"Right, Doc. Gotchya. Now give me the discharge please!" All this while, I could hear my roommate giggling from beneath his blankets and his pulse monitor was reading well into three digits. It was all I could do to keep a poker face. "And yes, Doc, I'll be certain to carry the vial of nitroglycerin tablets with me, too. Don't you worry. . ."

Justin picked me up at the hospital and the first thing he said after asking, "Hi Pop, how ya feelin'?" was, "Too bad today is Sunday and you can't get your hunting license." Bless his heart, he always did have a unique way with words and that statement was almost enough to make me take my first nitro pill.

"I'll get my license tomorrow, Partner, and we'll hunt the evening covey. . ." But, needless to say, Monday found me a bit too weak for any kind of hunt; thanks to the hospital food, I'd lost some 15-pounds and my strength was pretty much zapped. I wasn't too weak, however, to make the trip in to Wellsboro for my license. Barry, the owner of Davis' Sporting Goods, knowing of my recent bout with a heart that didn't work well, said, "You're gonna hunt after just having a heart attack? I knew all along that you, like most outdoor writers, were a bit weak in the mind, but I never. . ."

"Never what, Barry. Never knew we loved what we do and nothing short of Armageddon could stop us? If I can't hunt Barry, I might as well be dead! When I'm not hunting or fly-fishing or tying flies or writing about it all, I don't feel fully alive and it's my life's blood in more ways than one. Gotta do 'er, Barry and writing about it, which of course is sharing my experiences with others, is as important as the income I get from it. And that income, Barry, is what allows me to be one of your customers, reluctant as I am most of the time!"

Barry laughed and said, "You are a nutcase. Sit down here and fill out the application … need some shells?"

"Yes! Give Nutcase here a box of twelve-bore seven-and-a-halfs and a jug of that FP-Ten Lubricant. And Barry, bet your best boots I'm gonna plug you into my next story and let the world know how you treat your customers. Especially the outdoor writers! Nutcase! Ya know, oftentimes people will ask me what I love most, the outdoor life or the writing about it. Best way I could ever answer that was to come back with a question of my own asking which of their children they loved best. That usually ends it and I think it's always given them a clearer understanding of what we writers are all about. The whole thing is one, wonderfully priceless package and if indeed I'm gonna die, Barry, it'll be at the typer or in the woods."

Late that afternoon, weakness and all, I chose to give it a try. My wife Linda and daughter Erika helped me lace my boots. Justin filled the shell-loops in my orange vest—and graciously, I provided all the huffing and puffing as though I were doing all the work.

I was so very anxious to taste of the beautiful woodland across the road from our old farmhouse for, certainly, after more than forty years of hunting, that first hunt in early autumn becomes a psychological and coronary addiction. But, this late afternoon I simply couldn't make the grade through the field leading to the woods and grouse cover. I turned to see Justin's progress and noticed he was about 35-yards to my right and lagging behind somewhat. "What's the matter, Partner, can't keep up with the old man, huh?" And, God having blessed me with eyesight like an eagle, I saw that his eyes were glistening—noticeably. . .

"Pop," he said, shaking his head from side to side, "you just can't do this yet. Give it up for today, will ya? Why before, you'd have been to the woods by now. Just look at ya, puffing like an old steam engine! Hunting today isn't worth dyin' over is it?"

Jokingly, I answered, "Well, kinda. We've not missed a first day since you were twelve. I'm fine, just a little weak is all. C'mon, let's get going. We only have an hour or so as it is."

Justin said, "I'm heading for the barn, Pop. I'm just not in the mood to hunt today." And with that, he turned and walked back down the hill toward the house, turning every few steps to see if I was following. I looked to the woods, to him—then back to the woods again—and I suppose his companionship meant more to me than the hunt itself, so I followed him to the house. On the way, I vividly recalled something a Native American once said: "It seems to me that only leaves possess the secret of a beautiful death. . ."

Justin was right. The old autumn heart wasn't quite up to it all yet and would need some time, however little, to recover and I knew it would. . .

I'm not at all ashamed to admit to believing in Santa Claus, and small miracles, outdoor writer or not. I've been witness to a miracle or two in my time, depending, of course, upon how one defines "miracle." What follows is what I would place in the category of small miracles but one of paramount importance in my life.

That next morning, Justin and I, with my insistence, got an early start which, honestly, is not necessary for the grouse hunter. But the old man was anxious to fill his lungs with the smell of decaying leaves and, with any luck, the steely smell of grouse blood.

Most of my life, I've avoided medicines of any kind, including aspirin, which may have, with the help of say, 35 cigarettes a day, generously contributed to my heart attack? But before I left the hospital, the doc gave me a list of prescriptions as long as my arm and the various instructions indicated I was to take a total of 12 pills a day! I asked the doc, "Would it be okay if I just made a sandwich or a salad with them?" He laughed, I didn't. . .

Among the prescription medicines was the customary heart patient's sublingual, nitroglycerin tablets which I was to carry at all times. These things are about the size of an overweight germ with the power of a .357 magnum insofar as dilating blood vessels. Still, it's pretty hard changing the habits of a 54-year old man, be they bad or good ones but I've not had a single smoke since "The Day"—nor have I gotten used to toting those tiny nitro pills. . .

I told Justin to go into the far end of the woods and that I'd meet him later on. "You gonna be okay, Pop?"

"Do I look okay, Partner? Hey, I'm huntin' and that's the tonic of Nature. Just the ticket for an old autumn heart. Meet ya at the old flattop oak in about two hours." That meeting could have been one that never happened, for at the time I hadn't realized I'd forgotten my nitro pills. . .

Slowly, I began stillhunting, what I do best and best love, but hunting grouse without the aid of a dog before and after the shooting is like pulling a well-rooted tooth without the aid of pliers. Nevertheless, up the hollow I went with all the hope in the world tucked into my pocket, breathing in as deeply as possible that pungent air caused by rotting forest litter. "Better than Chanel Number Five," I thought.

With the gun nearly mounted on my shoulder, I worked my way through some promising cover and it wasn't long until I felt some pain in my chest. As it intensified a bit, I decided it wouldn't hurt to dissolve a nitro tab beneath my tongue; even though I felt the pain was born of anxiety? Wrong again, old man.

I sat down on a mossy deadfall and reached into my pants' pocket for my nitro and discovered I'd either lost them or left them on my desk at home. The pain remained stable and I could feel a little fear simmering in the same area. . .

As I indicated, we haven't a gun dog but we are owned by one remarkably intelligent, deeply affectionate and lovable German Shepherd mix. I've never been witness to a love any deeper than his for all members of our family and the depth of his numerous instincts are truly small miracles. He just seems to know things a dog shouldn't. . .

Sitting there amused by a multitude of gray squirrels, I nearly forgot about the chest pains when I heard something that sounded rather large shuffling toward my position. "Deer?" I thought. But, no. The rhythm wasn't quite right and after more than forty years as a hunter, one becomes pretty adept at identifying sounds of the forest. And this thing, whatever it was, seemed to be working in a meandering pattern—or so it sounded.

A moment or so later, I saw a large, black form scenting my trail through the oak shoots, more tight to the ground. "A bear?" I thought aloud. And, seconds later it indeed turned out to be a bear; a special one, for it was our family dog whose name happens to be, Bear!

But, never in the years we've had him (or him, us!) was he allowed to run alone or off the leash, save for Frisbee games. I whistled him up just about the time he'd spotted me and he came running, wearing that ever-present "smile" of his which displays his huge, white canines. He cried as we hugged and I asked, "What in the heck did ya do, Bear, break your chain?" he pulled away from me as though he wanted me to see what was tied to his collar and I swear, the look in his loving, hazel eyes seemed urgent.

"Whatchya got there big buddy, a sock?" He licked my wet, flushed cheeks as I untied the sock of nylon from his collar. Inside were my nitroglycerin tablets. I figured my wife had sent him to find me and later learned I was right.

I sat there holding the tiny bottle of pills and rubbing Bear behind his velvet ears. He barked, almost pleadingly, as though he wanted me to take the medicine. When I took one from the bottle, he stopped and soon thereafter, so did my chest pains. . .

That was the end of the day's hunt and I admitted, to myself, that I just wasn't quite up to it yet; Justin was right. "C'mon, Bear Dog, let's head for the barn!" He barked and led the way. "Ain't nothing gonna die today, Big Buddy. Me or a grouse. Maybe tomorrow though, huh Bear? Maybe tomorrow, if I can just keep the batteries running in this old autumn heart of mine. . ."

Once again, I realized that something I've always told my children was truer than I originally thought. That being, it's not the destination that makes life a joy worth living, it's the journey itself—and it doesn't hurt one bit to have a Bear to share it with, gun dog or not. . .

Perhaps because of Bear's loving effort whereby he found me, I'll live to hunt, not only the morning covey, but next autumn's as well? And, having a hero I'm told, adds to one's longevity—Bear's mine. And forever shall be....

AUTHOR'S NOTE: Every dog owner feels his dog is or was the best, ever, which indeed, is how it should be, always. They are not "made special" by their human counterparts, their "owners", but come that way from a special corner of Canine Heaven, that place I pray God allows me to go when I leave this crazy planet. Tippy and I have a lot of unfinished business and too, I'd like to know whether she felt me kissing her goodbye; it's been bothering me for far too long a time. I'd almost bet my old Fox Sterlingworth, she'll be the one to answer the door, for she was always there first when I came home here on Earth… Tippy was the best, blue-collar or not…

## "Tip's Last Bunny"

I've always leaned toward the blue-collar side of life. Partly because my income demanded it, but moreover, because there's nothing fancy about me or my demeanor. You surely know the type? When everyone at a splendid black-tie affair wears tails and stiff, white collars, I show up, happier than a Brittany with a snootful of grouse feathers to sniff, wearing a worn corduroy jacket with worn, leather elbow patches and fairly new jeans with, at least a razor-sharp crease. I suppose most would label me the "Vagrant-looking Non-conformist?"

Being the simple man God made me, I even prefer those dogs that come in a plain, brown wrapper and I do love dogs. And that is what this story is about; a dog…

Being an outdoor writer, there was considerable peer pressure put upon me with regard to owning a dog of the hunting type. Most of my gunning writer acquaintances each, at one time or another, either owned a legendary gun dog—or hunted over them frequently...

Of course, I wanted to make at least a tenuous attempt at keeping up with the gunning writers who hunted over fabled gun dogs and even with my ardent taste for the inelegant and distaste for status quo objects, living or otherwise, I was driven by peer pressure to go out and search for one who would own me—without being ashamed...

Ultimately, I forked out a forty dollar bill and no, obviously I didn't splurge on an elite Brittany spaniel in lemon and buff! Nor did I give one of the marvelous Chesapeake Bay retrievers an opportunity to own me; keep in mind here that my taste is pedestrian and I'm a blue-collar kind of guy... And truly, the dog was as much a birthday present to my then, ten-year old son, Justin, as it was a very weak attempt at gaining status among my faction of writers. So, I bought a beagle. And even though as a pup she was vividly reminiscent of a stream-lined piglet, she came chockful of love, loyalty, and that heavenly canine manner of understanding, and certainly fit my lifestyle to the proverbial "tee."

Legendary writer Gene Hill once owned a fine Lab, an ebony sweetheart named, "Tippy." She passed on quite some time ago and I felt she no longer needed the use of her name except in Gene's prayers, so I asked him whether he'd mind should I name our new blue-collared beagle, "Tippy." Gene, gracious gentleman he is, wrote me back saying, "Joseph: My best to Tippy-Two. It's a grand old name and carries a tradition of canine irresponsibility—wait and see! I once named a Lab of mine, Ed Zern, to flatter him (Zern) but it was a terrible retriever and I sold it and the owner changed the name... Let the dog chew on your shoe—She'd give you hers if you wanted to chew on it. Best, Gene."

And, so it went, our new beagle became Tippy-Two, Tippy for short, and if you're laughing here, imagine the sentiments of Gene when he learned of my wanting to name a blue-collar beagle after his world-class, and famous Lab. But, good old Hilly spared me the insult of what he "may"

144

have been thinking. Of course, the phrase "class-act" didn't come into the English language until Gene Hill became known to the American people...He's a gentleman, top shelf and then some.

Tippy, the 40-dollar beagle, besides being a bundle of fathomless love, had a scenting ability that surpassed "astounding." She nurtured this propensity to thoroughly please us that was so wondrous, so unyielding, so determined it had to hurt her physically. But she always seemed as though she enjoyed her efforts, in such a way that she made pleasure out of what had to be tough work for a little dog of eighteen pounds?

She always tried to love each member of the family equally and would forever run from one to the other kissing and licking our faces as though she kept count; three for Dad, three for Mom, three for Justin and three for Erika. And always her count came out just right.

Tippy could've kicked butt in any field trial, but I don't believe in that kind of stress being put on a dog intended for a pet. We were content to have her nearby, snoring at the foot of our beds each night. And I was more than content with her undiluted devotion and the occasional rabbit off her circling chases. Hilly would have loved her, world class in her own loving way. For a simple rub behind her velvety ears, a small display of love, she'd give it back a thousand-fold.

Sometimes we'd have to leave her alone in the house for an hour or a few, and when we'd return, one would think we were gone for months! She cried so loudly, that once an obnoxious neighbor, who obviously knew nothing of how much hounds adore humans, phoned the Human Society on us, thinking we were abusing her. Perhaps we were, for we hugged her very long and hard after arriving home...

Once on an outing in the Endless Mountains of Pennsylvania, we stopped to rest and walk. Tippy tore, enthusiastically toward a trout stream without one of us at her side. No doubt thirsty from the confinement of the family wagon? About the time I saw her reach the creek, I heard her

145

cry out loudly and I ran to her side to see what happened. Immediately, she favored her right, front paw and was noticeably limping. I scooped her into my arms and carried her to the wagon where I checked her out thoroughly. I scrutinized every inch of her body, legs and even tail as she cried in pain. Over and over and over and nothing! Not a mark, nor a hair out of place anywhere. And, to this very day, we know not what happened that day at the creek's edge. All we really, and sadly, knew is from that day forward her health failed progressively—and far too fast...

I knew somehow, because of a terrible gut feeling, I was going to lose a symbol of love, a legendary hunting companion, and yes, a member of the family I loved as well as any. I somehow knew my children would soon be losing their guardian, their second mother, and a little dog that may well kill a stranger for messing with "her" children... In the area of protection of my children, our Tippy was then and only then, an animal...

The vet said she had cancer, though I never believed him. He gave her but six months; "best scenario..." Six more months to share with us. To love us to no limit and the reverse of that, us loving her to no end. Six more months perhaps, to snore at the foot of our beds, to cry when we came home and show dreadful hurt in her wonderful, hazel eyes at our leaving—even though she knew it would be but a short time. 'My dear God," I said, dying a little each day myself, "She has a year's supply of doggie treats we bought her before the news." I guess, though, He needed her? Perhaps to prod the derriere of a fleeing, hell-bent for cover cottontail? "So," I thought, "God's a blue-collar kind of 'guy' too?" I had to wonder as a means by which to divert my thoughts from what was so painfully obvious. But we had one hell of a time living with Tip dying and it was easy to see the hurt in our eyes, especially the children's.

I recall many nights of prayer. "Please God, if you would, just show me the way to make the remainder of Tippy's life totally wonderful, completely full. I want her to realize every joy she's ever dreamed of, please..."

Months passed and Tip grew visibly and terribly worse. I pleaded with my wife to let me put her down, so she could at least retain the marvelous pride of hers, but no. My children and her (and I) wanted so much, to hold on just a little while longer. There were countless times when I wanted to die in her place but I knew that kind of thinking was irrational, foolish and unsound. Sure, Tip could protect the children and did, but she couldn't provide for them. Time after time I asked them to, "Let go. It's best for Tippy." All the while feigning my own tenacious reluctance…

One warm, May morning I had to leave my office at a large lumber company where I was the purchasing agent and run an errand which would take me to town and past the house. As I passed the front of our house, I noticed Tip was lying on the porch soaking in the heat of the morning sun; she so loved doing that. She looked pitiful lying there on her side, bloated with cancer and devoid of her once cherished rambunctiousness. That which she had an unusual abundance of in those sweet, not-so-long-ago days. She was just over six years old now, and that lack of life and energy had to be terribly confusing to her?

I stopped the truck in the middle of the street and ran to her side. She was all but gone and with her half-closed eyes, seemed to be looking to the sun for help? I didn't know. Perhaps in some magical language between dog and Universal Energy, she asked for a little more time, but a moment or two? Maybe Tippy felt she could absorb some of the sun's abundant, solar energy into her own, now nearly lifeless, 18 pound mass? It was so obvious in those sienna, hazel eyes, she simply wanted more time. Time to love us, time to protect the children one more day, and certainly time to feel the love of our patting hands just once more? And I knew, all too well, the sun was denying her very last personal wish. Possibly, the only thing she ever wished for…

I ran into the house and grabbed my shotgun and two number six shot shells. My wife intercepted me on my way back through the living room, "What in the world are you going to do?"

"I'm taking Tippy for one last hunt, that's what!"

Rabbits are legal game year-round in Eastern Oregon, but for Tippy I would break more than laws. I lifted her, cradling her limp body in my arms and headed to the truck, still in the middle of the street. She was holding on courageously, but by a fast-weakening golden thread weaved of silken love and simply because she wanted to stick around. To love us, take care of us and yes, cry for us when we were occasionally forced to leave her behind.

Perhaps Tip felt she was somehow betraying us but, "No Tippy, we know better than that..." She was top-shelf in the loyal category and showed us more love and devotion than any human deserves. A love so deep, strong and genuine, that she hung on for almost six months longer than the vet initially gave her. Although in a physical state I thought must be painful? She just refused to submit to her enemy cancer, and deeply concerned for her comfort, I asked the doc if cancer was painful. He said something like, "...only to those living with and loving the victim and watching them die little by little." He was right about that... And even though Tippy outlived the 6-months or less prediction by the vet, and was for the most part, lethargic, she always had the energy to show her love and weakly wag her tail when we spoke with her. She was magical and tough and I couldn't have asked for a more prestigious dog or friend, Heaven knows...

I drove Tip to the high desert just outside of town, to a place right on the famous Oregon Trail. There were rabbits there and she loved the scent of rabbits, sage and unbound freedom and space. Perhaps even more than the occasional steak we'd cook up for her in spite of my blue-collar wages. In life, rabbit scent and the taste of spaghetti were her favorite things. I always felt she carried some of my ancestral, Italian blood in her veins.

"Tippy," I said as we drove to the edge of town, "You're not quite up to chasing bunnies today, so I'll take care of it for you." We left the truck and I had to carry her cradled in my left arm until it became numb from lack of circulation. She was so relaxed, and her little, well-defined head bobbed with every step as we hunted up a bunny. She licked several times, at the backside of my hand, as though she was apologizing for being such a burden. I summoned a long-ago song I liked: "You ain't heavy Tippy, you're my sweetheart…"

The May desert sun had me sweating heavily but after about 30-minutes we flushed a bunny and I cut loose from the hip hurriedly, with my old Fox double. The rabbit rolled to a dusty stop and I retrieved it for my Tip.

As I lifted the rabbit to her dry nose, she looked into my eyes with hers almost open wide. As if to say, "I'm sorry, I just can't help you anymore, Boss. Wish I could…"

I walked with her to a flat rock where we could sit and share what I knew would be Tip's last bunny. I set the rabbit down, and then placed Tip right next to it so she could bury her wonderful nose deeply into the scent-filled fur. Then I left her to walk the 50-yards or so to the truck for the shovel. Knowing all the while she was leaving but wouldn't without first saying "goodbye" to me. We were friends, save those painful times I had to be disciplinarian. But, even then, I think Tippy understood I loved her regardless.

As I walked back to her, the sage seemed to bring flooding to my eyes. But through the glistening, I could see that Tip had placed one paw upon her bunny. When I reached her, she was breathing, but laboriously. I just sat there. At a loss for appropriate words. And completely unsure of what I could do to ease her passing. In a few moments, Tippy left me for wherever it is God takes his greatest creations. Although I don't know, I'd like to think she felt me kiss her head that one, last time. And I still hope that, today, some five years later…

I moved the large rock and dug the deepest hole, where it rested. I went to the truck for her little, but elaborate casket; one I'd made months prior. I said my "So long," and placed her into the deep grave where I somehow knew she wouldn't be for long.

After covering it all and replacing the large, shale-like rock, I used a stone to inscribe three little words on the big rock covering Tip's grave. They said, for I knew she'd approve, "We Love You." Simple, but appropriate for a plain, brown wrapper, blue-collar dog?

They say in ignorance, that time heals all wounds. That's the worst of one-line jokes. Time merely hides the wound—covers it with a scarring just enough that it doesn't show all that much—at least when we speak of losing a dog, hunting breed or otherwise...

I'm still the blue-collar guy I mentioned previously, in fact, with Tippy gone, a little poorer than ever before. She was the only real wealth I'd ever known. And no, I'll never allow another hunting dog to adopt me.

However, we have another member of the family, acquired since Tip's departure. A sort of remarkable mutt, half shepherd with some Rottweiler and collie. Bear, we call him, and a dog more full of love lies beneath a rock on Virtue Flats in eastern Oregon for I honestly doubt there's a dog on Earth that loves more than Bear? His full name is Bear D. Dawg...

Is Bear a replacement for Tippy? Of course not. You can't replace lost love and devotion like she gave. You merely supplement as best you can with another dog and hope like hell it buffers some of your pain, however little.

Do we love Bear as much as we did, Tip? Certainly. But differently. And he loves us to where it sometimes appears to hurt him, crying when we come home just like Tippy did. Did I ever take Bear to the grave where Tippy sleeps forever? Yes, once. Did he sniff the gravesite and weep as legend says? No. But I honestly feel he wanted to when he saw my mood. But then, how could he know how I was hurting? Who knows? All I do know is that he appeared very sad as I spoke to Tippy that day. Dogs are funny like that, that is if you think of depth and celestial, extra-sensory instinct, as "funny." Personally, I don't but instead, cherish it as something very special in Life.

Of Life's joys, few if any, equal the joy and love shared between man and dog. I thank God everyday of my life that my wife understands that, but then it was Tippy who taught her to understand that kind of love. And a grand job she did.

In that sense, Tippy will live on, forever. And, not too long from now, I'll rustle her up another bunny which may be her first in a place where good things never die...

AUTHOR'S NOTE: The gun in this story was far and away, my father's greatest material love. The night before he passed on, while lying in an intensive care unit of a San Diego hospital, trying so hard not to slip away, he asked my stepmother just before she left his bedside, "Honey, is my Colt still in the safe deposit box at the bank?" And it was, though Pap would never again fondle it, twirl it or just sit and gaze at it like a kid might gaze at a moon rock.

Without a doubt, this single-six is one of the most breathtaking guns I've ever held or seen. Pap always said, "When I die, Joey, this'll be yours to give to Justin." And as the story tells, he did and I did and Justin, my 22-year old son is now the very proud owner of his grandfather's most prized possession. Although we rarely take it out to look at it any more, we know it's there and in a strange but warm sense, it's like knowing a part of my father is still with us, Justin's grandfather; the only "hero" Justin's ever had in his young life.

Believe it or not, this Peacemaker traveled home with us after we'd buried Pap. I suppose the look in my eyes as I explained the circumstances to the airline clerk convinced him to give it special care in the baggage compartment of the 757? I would have piled in down under the passenger cabin to be with it but special arrangements were made for the Colt, thank goodness. . .

And Pap, if you're reading this, I know you'll know it's in possession of someone who will love it even **more** than you did. And Pap? Thanks. . .

## "A Requiem By Peacemaker"

After more than fifty years of living, I've never been able to make any sense of death or come to any certain terms with it. It is too large, too harsh in its nakedness. Death has always caused my thoughts to run rampant, eventually taking me right back to where I started in my attempts to get it squared away in my aging mind.

Death to me is pretty much the same whether on the home front and personal level or in the autumn hunting fields. Though death in the hunting fields is less painful for the most part, it is still confusing. But at least there it's bittersweet. As hunters, we all know the feeling I speak of: remorse with a dash of "sugar" to remove most of the bitter "taste." Most of us know that the best way for an animal to die is by the well-placed hunter's bullet, far more merciful than time and heartless Mother Nature.

At least there in the fields or woodlands, there's some privacy for the emotion we may experience at the moment of death—our kill. With the death of a loved one, however, there is seldom any privacy when the realization of the tragedy hits us. It carves out emotional agony, well-etched onto our faces, a place where it cannot be concealed. And yes, it **always** hurts, for indeed death is terribly abrupt and clearly final. Because of these facts of life on Earth, abstract and perplexing and repulsive as they certainly are, at each ethereal sunrise I rediscover the very precious nature of Life, even with all of its complexities and strangeness. Living, in a sense, is Man's natural, God-given wealth, a wondrous value for the paltry price we sometimes have to pay for it, if indeed we take the time and always evaluate the true worth of it. And, so it goes. We try to do what we can to make death seem okay, or within our hearts, justify it.

And is it not a curious oar that so vigorously stirs a man's ardent desire to somehow honor the deceased after the hurtful fact? Is this, perhaps, the way the living function in an effort to feel at least a tad better about their loss? Certainly, the best we can do for the dead is to "let them go." Still, it's somehow acceptable to perhaps cling to their dreams, nurture them and ultimately try to fulfill them. Then try to be satisfied that you've done your very best to find peace in the seemingly meaningless and confusing finality of it all. It's contentment, however small, and consoling comes from doing so. I know. . .

When my father, whom we referred to as "Pap," died, I experienced a relentless need to fill at least one of **his** small, lifelong dreams. For so, so long I harbored this burning propensity to immortalize him with something I knew he wanted while living but never got. But 'how' was the toughest part of that desire. And setting things in motion caused me to constantly daydream, wondering just what it might be? The best I could come up with was to bestow the full honor and dignity to his most prized possession. A fully engraved Colt single-action Army revolver in .32-20 Winchester caliber. A masterpiece of craftsmanship and beauty that has left many calloused hunter acquaintances of mine breathless and visibly starry-eyed. This gun was the second love in his life and he called it his Peacemaker. Now, even though I wish he were still here to call it his, it's mine—or was.

My feelings were, that to do honor to something he loved literally to his dying day would be paying tribute to him, thus honoring his ever-present memory. In a sense, keeping Pap alive in spirit at least. Other than this, I tried to console myself with thinking as the Shoshone tribe of the Wind River Reservation had taught me long ago. That is, "there is no death but rather a change of worlds. . ."

The Peacemaker idea seemed fitting but I, not all that proficient with a handgun at the time, wondered just how I would accomplish it. I'm a rifleman to the very marrow of my bones, a lover of the long guns and, at best, fair with the pistols we own. Indeed, the thought of the ballistics charted for the .32-20 gripped me by the throat, knowing I'd have to get an uncommonly close shot, say 35-yards or less for the instant kill. And I knew old Pap would only "settle" for and accept a whitetailed buck to bring honor to his beloved Peacemaker. I found myself smiling as I wondered and pictured him sitting on some celestial perch, a front row seat, laughing at all of this nonsense I'd come up with. I could almost hear him reminding me as he always did in my younger days as a hunter: "If there's a trace of doubt about the shot, Joey, don't pull the trigger. One shot, one kill, or nothing. . ."

I asked my son, Justin, "How do you think I could honor Pap's Peacemaker, Partner?"

Justin looked at me with that "You ought to know glare" in his big, hazel eyes and answered me without a second's hesitation or speculation: "Simple, Pop. Ya gotta kill with it. It's the **only** way, you know that! And you also know the only thing that will make it just right is a whitetailed buck!" Blood of my blood, flesh of my flesh, he not only thinks as his father, he is able to read his father's mind? But, sure, he was right. Drawing blood with any gun is, was, and forever shall be the ultimate honor to the gun. Long barrel, short barrel or two-barrel, it must be the most intimate part of the hunting ritual with regard to the culmination, if indeed a kill is intended.

The Second World War from Bastogne, to the Rhine crossing, to the landing on Normandy on that bloodiest of June days had, I know, well-removed Pap's desire to kill— anything. He simply loved the hunt and all the mystery and romance that went with being in the big woods. His "need" to draw blood, perhaps even his emotional tolerance for it, long ago died in his veteran heart.

How well, though, I can recall those days after the war when he'd talk of how his dreams used to be centered around his taking a whitetailed buck with his .300 Savage. "Used to fire my favorite dreams, Joey, takin' a buck with my model 99, but now? Hell, son, I don't know. . ." And no. He never brought himself to make his dream come true. So, I, his eldest son, chose to live it for him. Crazy? I suppose, but nevertheless, this idea now fired my dreams.

I sat there kneading the oiled, walnut grips of the Peacemaker. Staring off into the prospective Killing Wood like a daydreaming child. It is just a few hundred yards from the house, this whitetail-ridden hollow, and certainly I know the deer well, but still. I wished at the time I could have, by some sort of bizarre form of telepathy, placed the Peacemaker into a state of metamorphosis, perhaps into a

155

walking staff which I might use to walk away from all this "Filler-Of-Dreams" insanity. But I couldn't and all the while, knew it. The relentless, primordial chanting inside of me, singing, "Go, go, go. . ."

That ancestral atavistic savage who inwardly haunts my unpretentious way of life and lifts me to the hunts of autumn is now, and was then, one merciless and convincing power. On those days just prior to the hunting seasons, "he" seems to emerge from a state of suspended animation and begin his omniscient, ravenous pleading, as if to plead with me, or taunt me, in a sort of beckoning manner just to satisfy "his" needs. Perhaps "his" coming to "life" is triggered by the passing of the sun over the equator which causes autumn, a changing of the worldly guard? His incessant begging, so convincing, is like precision clockwork; and "he's" been that way for over four decades now. I've yet been unable to stave off the percolating, predatory urges that simmer way down deep and this time, anticipating the hunt with Pap's Peacemaker, emotions were no different except for my confidence level, with the idea of using a handgun. It was in serious decline. . .

I pondered and pondered the idea, wanting to chuck it all. But my ears nearly rang with the deep desire and finally, after a long time of fondling Pap's greatest material love, I answered the pesky little savage spirit in the affirmative. Not so much for "his" satisfaction this time, but for mine, for Pap's. And so, I became submissive once again, to the relentless, spiritual champion and decided I should, "Go, go, go. . ."

An ebony Crayola and a paper plate of about 8-inches, along with a quarter have always served me well for making targets. To my mind, store-bought targets are an ignorant extravagance. I use the quarter to outline the bulls-eye circle, just larger than an inch, then color it in and slide the two-bits back into my jeans—where it belongs. My thinking? A thrifty shooter will always be the best shooter. For example, he'll pick his one best shot at an animal and kill it. With the target idea, it becomes prudent in that he'll still have a pocketful of quarters for coffee money and maybe even enough for a cinnamon donut?

My daughter, Erika, is the family Picasso, though a far better "artist." She's also the "producer" of targets. "Erika! Please make me up a few targets, honey! And use your own quarter!" She's become a well-learned student of her mother's, rarely returning my quarters and after several times, I got wise. I'm not tight, mind you, just thrifty!

At nearly $20 per box for 100-grain cartridges, I knew this sighting-in exercise would be considerably short. Right? Wrong! After the gorgeous (looks aren't everything, remember?) Colt belched out the first half-dozen rounds, I could have poured mother's beef broth into the belly of the paper plate and not worried about a drop of leakage!

"Good grief!" I thought, looking at the plate. I then examined the Peacemaker as though it were at fault. "How long are you going to continue **this** nonsense?" Tighter bead this time, 6-o'clock hold and bingo! Six more rounds fired. Two in the plate but absolutely no understanding as to why the other 4 flew elsewhere. Next six. Little tighter bead this time, steady two-hand hold, breathe—exhale a whiff and squeeze. Better; four in the center and two wherever it is little spheres of lead go when they're not imbedded in the wood behind one's target? After a number of rounds, which I herein refuse to disclose for reputation's sake, I had the Peacemaker printing well enough to make Orion the Hunter's eyes water. Give or take a "flyer," the groups were consistently under the three inches I wanted. Pleased? Yes, but still quite apprehensive about the task that lay before me.
. .

The nagging indweller would soon be at peace, I hoped. My targets certainly enhanced my confidence level and his ardent need, which in naked reality was my own, would soon be satisfied. I went to the shed to tinker, wishing the hunt could be the usual, with my old Ruger '06, but knowing in my hunting heart that the requiem by his Peacemaker had to transpire; my desire now too deep, too strong, to dispel.

Justin walked into the shed and picked up an unused target, then casually questioned me, "So, this is it, huh, Pop?" I looked at him threateningly over the top of my glasses then pointed to the punched target pinned to a rafter above his head.

"No! That's it above your ligneous head!"

"How far?" He asked.

"Twenty-five well-stretched steps!"

"Well, Pop, that ought to do 'er. But, you know? You ought to give some serious thought to hunting from a tree stand. It'd be to your advantage and maybe get ya a closer shot than you really need? What's ligneous, by the way?"

"Never mind ligneous," I said, trying to act at though his furtive idea meant little to me. "You just may be right though, about the stand idea. I'll give it some thought."

Near the edge of the hardwoods stood an ancient tree stand. Weather-beaten, yet inviting because of its location and sturdy looking construction. It looked as though it might work just fine for the hunt, the strategy I planned to employ.

There had to have been some incredible history behind this old structure and the old Colt and I just might add some "color" to it. Lingering elements had taken their toll, and heavily, on the old platform section, but the steps were still alive with spring and strength. I decided I'd climb them and make the needed repairs before buck season, which is what I ultimately did. I went so far as to build a windbreak around its perimeter.

Little Orphan Creek was trilling innocently as I sat on the perch after I'd finished, nursing a bowlful of China Black Whiskey blend pipe tobacco. Squirrels scurried about the mossy forest floor below, through the duff and tapestry. Nature's very own carpeting, like the shadows of miniature clouds; so quiet, it was hard to believe they were actually moving. A pileated woodpecker flitted from tree to tree and I couldn't help but marvel at the quiet speed he was able to gain with just a gentle urging of a wingbeat. I envied so his freedom, his ability to fly. Some of Man's most pleasurable dreams are of flying—if only once. . .

A widowed dove mourning from a nearby, lone hemlock, seemed to fix her stare upon my position. "Coo-ah, coo-ah, coo, coo, coo," she sang. I wondered if this was her subtle way of scolding me for the intrusion or was her dulcet, little, melancholy song carrying a message for me? Crazy, what runs through a man's mind during times like these. But there was such a brokenheartedness to her wild tongue and the plangent, rhythmic song was haunting. "I guess she could be trying to tell me something?" I thought aloud. Her mourning was so incessant it **had** to mean something other than just everyday sentiments, so, I answered her as though, yes, I understood. As I climbed down from the tree, I said to her, "A man's gotta do, sweetheart, what a man's gotta do." Her song stopped just about the time my feet hit the ground. As though it was her way of saying, "Okay, why listen to me?"

Who knows, save for our Creator? Still, I left the area feeling less predatory than ever before in my life, which is akin to Robert Ruark saying, "I hate African safaris." Wild places are magical though, and we who hunt know that stranger things happen out there than anywhere else on earth. And if it felt to me as though this little dove was trying to tell me something, so be it. And if I was feeling a little less predatory than usual, that's okay too. And indeed I was.

Walking home, I wondered whether biologists actually believe what they are taught, that animals are incapable of displaying emotion or demonstrating logic? I believe they can and do and I'm an avid biologist though self-taught. Think about the robins that stoop from the tree near the house trying to frighten those who come too close to their nesting site? That's a defensive instinct, yes, but certainly done for the protection of their young, out of an emotion called love. And how about their constant trips back and forth from the nest as they labor by carrying food for their brood. My feeling is they're thinking something similar to, "Hey, the kids must eat and I must provide." Precisely what must run through their BB-sized brains? Then there's the pride of lions in Africa I once saw which convinced me, almost completely. The entire pride actually bawled when one of their "loved" ones perished after being gored by a Cape Buffalo. That's grief, no matter how one slices it and that, too, is an emotion. Closer to home, let us look at the precious, little killdeer bird, a shore bird to be sure, but one who frequents the inland bottomlands of farms. Go anywhere near their ground nests and they'll feign a broken wing and attempt to lead you from the nesting site. What might we call that? Not dramatic acting to be sure, but sheer intelligence, a protective diversionary measure much closer to something called logic?

So, if we watch and listen carefully, wildlife may very well "speak" to us on occasion, through body language or by some other means, and, if we are fortunate, we may even understand it from time to time. To my mind and heart, the little dove had spoken to me, personally, and somehow, just somehow mind you, I felt I understood her. Titillating sounds pour not from the vocal chords of a dove and I knew it. And this one's melancholy "coo-ah, coo-ah, coo, coo, coo" was somehow special, somehow telling me **something** special. Little did I know, I would heed her rather sad melodious "request" and as I walked toward home, it was pretty clear just what I had to do—if and when. . .

Not 25-yards from the stand's ladder base was a buck rub, a fairly good one and certainly not that of an immature, sapling buck. I recall whispering to myself, "There's the sign. Everything seems to be falling into place. . ." Mainly due to the fact that there were several other rubs not far from the one near the stand-site. "The Red Gods are smiling. . ."

My son, Justin, was shooting hoops in the yard as I walked up on him. "Heck of a buck runnin' the hollow this year, Justin!"

"Yep!" he said, "And he's an eight-pointer, too! I saw him in that stand of birches yesterday."

"Why didn't you say something then?"

"A to Z, Pop, it's your hunt. I knew you'd find him on your own and besides, remember when I was a kid you always said that the more personal effort a guy puts into a hunt, the more gratification he gets from it?" And yes, he was right. This hunt was created by the desire to bring honor to Pap's Colt, to pay tribute to him and it was my hunt, and my choice.

"Yeah, reckon you're right, partner. Thanks for gettin' me back on track. Heck of a nice buck though, huh?"

"I also recall your telling me God makes 'em all nice, Pop!" My son well-remembered his earlier lessons from a guy many referred to as "The Preacher."

A few hours of stakeout in the stand, two one day, one the next and several another and I'd seen the buck twice. Only once within comfortable .32-20 range, about 35 yards. "Saw the buck this mornin', Justin!"

"Good, did he come in close?"

"Close enough the one time, 'bout thirty-five yards. We shouldn't have too much trouble, though. He's gotta make one mistake in two weeks of hunting season?"

Justin cocked his head, squinted one eye and, looking me square in the eyes, said, "What's this 'we' stuff, Pop? You got a mouse in your pocket?"

"No! But I'd sure like you to share this hunt with me, partner. Be nice, wouldn't it, to witness this hunt with your grandfather's Peacemaker? You know, something to tell your children when ol' Pop changes worlds. What do ya say?"

"What can I say, Pop? I'd feel like a cowpie if I didn't go along now!"

For days, I found myself seriously appraising that which was about to transpire. This hunt with Pap's Peacemaker wasn't about killing. It wasn't about bragging rights or challenge or glory, either. To my mind and heart, it was about honor. A tribute that should be paid to a fine man, and a fine gun. No. This hunt was about Life itself, and dignity. And the fulfilling of a dead father's dream that, somehow, still lived within me. Even though I'd built up my confidence by getting the Colt to print well, something deep inside of me was changing, baring the very pellicles of a predatory mind and an aging and mellowing heart. A hunter's heart?

I was forever questioning the actions I chose in the autumn woods. The killing of any animal always seemed remorseful, but I had to fill the needs of the instinct inside me, bittersweet or not. I decided to go through with my tenuous plans.

One evening I spotted the buck at the edge of our woods. He appeared to be staring right into my eyes from the 300-plus yards distance. We'd eyed each other for what seemed like several moments and, afterwards, I could only come to one accurate description of this animal—gorgeous. Calling this whitetail a "buck" was akin to calling Pope John Paul your "pastor." Or your Leonard cane flyrod your "fishin' pole." And I'm going to kill this buck? Maybe, maybe not. . .

The Sunday prior to the hunt, I came to the earth-shaking realization that I'd merely grown old and not up. I was as nervous and apprehensive as a child waiting in the lobby of a dentist and knew the night would allow me precious little sleep. And I was right.

By 5:45 A.M., Justin and I were in the stand sipping hot, cinnamon tea. I whispered, pointing to the colt, "I sure wish they'da made these things in 30-06!" and softly, we both laughed...

Justin nudged my leg with his and whispered, "Don't you worry, Pop. You'll do just fine if that ol' buck shows. The Peacemaker was never in **better** hands."

Pulling him in close and hugging him, I said, "Yeah, never in shakier hands either partner but thanks. Thanks a lot."

A few minutes after 8 a.m., Justin tapped my boot. Whispering, "Somethin' comin' in, Pop. 'Bout twelve o'clock." My pulse pounded furiously in my forearms but, as it turned out, it was four browsing does. They walked just beneath our stand and we noticed they were watching their backtrail. We looked in the direction of their attention and like a fog rising from a swamp bottom, he "materialized."

Just as I always told Justin. "They're like mushrooms, they just seem to burp up through the soil." Suddenly and quietly.

When we first spotted him, he was out about 40-yards but he was strolling in closer, completely unaware of us, but still with the customary cautious advancement. When he finally stopped at what I determined to be about 25-yards, I drew back the hammer of the Peacemaker, the sound reminiscent of tiny branches snapping, although fine and precision-like. His ears twitched, cupping like miniature radar units and he ever so gently stomped the ground. He seemed uncommonly bewildered, as though something wasn't quite right in his sylvan world, with his unparalleled instincts. He seemed, somehow, to know he was in trouble?

I raised the Colt to a tight bead just behind his head at the juncture of his muscular neck, held my breath, released a little air quietly and thought to myself, "Without a doubt, you're mine." I then stood quickly, thrust my arms out to their full extension and shouted as loud as possible, "Bang!" Immediately, or perhaps sooner than that, the big buck bolted, kicking up forest ground litter and spreading it well behind him, hell-bent for safer ground. I smiled as his vertical white flag bade us, "Farewell!"

"Pop! What in the heck did ya do that for, you had him dead to rights! Ain't **no** way you would have missed!" I looked at Justin, then in the direction the gorgeous buck had gone and smiled. Then Justin continued, "Pop, you **know** you could have killed him, right?"

"Yes, Partner, I sure do and without question. And that perhaps is the best we'll remember about this day, at least as far as I'm concerned. Knowing I could have but didn't, Justin. It was the way your grandfather hunted since he came home from the war and if it was good enough for Pap, then it's sure good enough for me. Come on, son, let's head home."

All through the alfalfa field we cross on our way home, Justin said, over and over, "I cannot believe you did that, Pop!" At the house I would explain but right then, I was still tasting the sweetness of the moments past.

At home, Justin and I sat to finish the thermosed tea. "Justin, what I did out there today in our tree stand was about honor and life. I allowed a life to go on when all I had to do was touch the trigger. That's what the old Peacemaker is all about isn't it? What better honor could I, a mortal being, a simple man, bestow on it than to allow a magnificent life like that buck's to continue when certainly I had the opposite choice? By golly, old Pap should be happy with that, don't you think?"

"You are one **crazy** father, Pop! I suppose that's why I love ya so doggone much."

"And I love you too, Son. Now, how's about you wiping down that Peacemaker while the old man here gets some shuteye? It's yours now, by the way. And always remember, Justin, there's a lot of love within that Colt. A lot. It's kinda like the wind. Ya can't see it but you sure can feel it."

And with that, I was almost gone. Dozing and content with my choice. I drifted into that magical hollow where dreams are realized and life goes on just as Pap may have liked it? I thought as I drifted off, "I'll call that little hollow Requiem Hollow, by God." Besides, giving away a gun as priceless as Pap's Peacemaker makes a man mighty doggone tired. . .

As I dozed off, I could hear Justin mumbling to himself at the dining room table just after I'd heard the loading gate of the Colt open and Justin turning the cylinder. "Jeez! Ol' Pop never even loaded the darn thing. . ."

With one eye cocked open, I watched a proud young man, a fine son, wiping down his grandfather's beloved Peacemaker and finally felt I understood death? Death is a thing from which the living draw their inspiration to carry on, to live, and celebrate life as though there may be no tomorrow. And on this day of The Requiem, Justin and I had indeed done just that.

AUTHOR'S NOTE: This piece was penned after Pap left us. He never got to read it, obviously, and it is a tribute to him, and other members of the Fighting 159th Combat Engineer Battalion. Without them, without Pap, this book, a longtime dream, never would have come to pass. They and hundreds of thousands of other soldiers fought, long and hard, so that you, and I, may live—hopefully making the world a better place. And so I could pen this story.

### "On War & Whitetails"

Many of us served our country in a time of peace. We then, are the fortunate. For it's beyond the mind's ability to vividly imagine how disturbing it would be to look a man in the eyes, then fire eight, thirty-caliber bullets into his writhing body; a total stranger. . .

However, in a sense, that's what a letter to countless Americans said they'd been chosen to do at the upstart of World War II. My father, as perhaps countless war veterans, could no doubt close his eyes and visualize every word in the frightening invitation?

Dad was but 22-years old when that letter beckoned him with strange words written only "between" the lines: "Go to this strange land and fight for your country." He had no enemies there, but his country did. And so, being a patriot to the very core and loving the unique American way of life, he left.

Dad, whom we later called Pap, like others who served in our nation's war efforts, must have experienced a great deal of despair and emotional discomfort and confusion. That is going to a land of strangers to fight them? Men, then the enemy, whom he may very well have befriended otherwise, perhaps breaking bread with them or hunting the whitetail in a friendlier forest. . .

I was around nine-months old when Dad handed me in my blue wrapping to my mother, then boarded the big ship for the European Theatre—give or take a hamper full of dirty diapers. Too young to know I should be crying at his leaving. Too young to realize his chances of taking me hunting on my 12th birthday were, at very best, slim. And I feel Dad wasn't too shallow of mind and heart to vividly understand he was headed for a Hell on Earth; a place that may swallow his young vibrant body, to never spit it out.

Grandfather told me once-upon-a-time, Dad's last words to him were, "I'll see you, Pap. I love you very, very much. And I'll be back to hunt those swamp pheasants and rabbits with you, so please, don't worry. . ." Both wept according to Pap's account. He didn't tell me this. I could just tell, for those times he and Dad spent hunting were times when they'd felt better than Life normally allowed. But, of course, when Dad left for the war, those precious times were on the very edge of Never Again.

Dad hit Omaha Beach on "D-Day". He'd received some 5 bronze battle stars and a few other combat commendations. In a terrible battle where his outfit was grossly outnumbered, he lost buddies who had their rabbit hunting days terminated by indiscriminate Nazi bullets. He fought in the Battle of the Bulge, Bastogne, the Ardennes and other major campaigns. A battle on Hill 313, he once told me, was one of his worst nightmares. He never really spoke of it, but a book dedicated to his outfit did. The odds against his small outfit being victorious in that battle were tremendous. Outnumbered greatly, their chances seemed, at best, hopeless. But, they won. They suffered but three casualties. One, a first lieutenant from Pittsburgh, Pennsylvania, Herbert O. Leckman, or "Big Moe" as his men called him. Dad was called "Little Moe" and their outfit was referred to as "The Fighting Moes" of the 159$^{th}$ Combat Engineers.

I asked him about Hill 313 and all he said was, ". . .that was a tough one, Joey." Dad and I talked mostly of hunting rabbits and pheasants and whitetails; the war was long over. He was home now.

Once, while we sat at the edge of a woodlot, I asked him a question regarding the war and his part. He never looked at me, but just stared straight ahead into the shady woods, seemingly caught up in his deep thought. He then revealed the story of a time when he'd shot his first Nazi soldier. It was as though he **needed** to set the thought free? A sort of therapy? I listened intently as he spoke softly, knowing from past accounts that his confirmed kills numbered some two digits, so why then, I thought, would he choose to tell me of a single, first kill?

"I carried an M-1 Garand then, Joey. It held a clip of eight rounds. We were out on re-con patrol one early evening and I spotted the German soldier standing against a tree which had a big "Y" just above the main trunk. His helmet silhouette gave him away as being the enemy. He was smoking a cigarette, and when he put it to his mouth and drew from it, I placed the sights right behind the glowing ash and cut loose. All eight rounds."

I never saw Dad look quite like he did that day. Never before saw his eyes tear. He continued his story: "Just as I was about to touch off those rounds, he turned to look me square in the eyes. It was the most hurtful thing I ever had to do. In battles, like Hill 313, you don't really see much, ya just shoot and hope and pray. No eyes looking back at you. Anyway, we were trained to search all enemy bodies, which I did with this youngster I'd just killed, and in his wallet were photos of him, his wife and two little girls. Together in that photo. Hell, Joey, that man wasn't any different than me. He, too, was there to do a horrible job, something neither of us really understood. Anyway, Son, that was my first time. And now you know. There just wasn't any satisfaction taking that man's life, that woman's husband and worse, the little girls' father. None. It was just a case of me or him, nothing personal about it. . ."

I shook my head as if to understand. But there's just no possible way of understanding something like that, that hurtful. For me or for my father.

Dad told me many times that all he did over there was try to stay alive and to bring his squad back home. He wanted to once again walk quietly through "needle-fine autumn rains" hunting with his father. He talked of how vividly he could remember while overseas, the laughs and times they shared while hunting together. "I knew," he said, "I just had to get back home. No matter what it took and God, my constant foxhole companion, saw to it that I did. . ." I was grateful, too, for it gave me a chance to share many wonderful days in the hunting fields with a father. Some kids weren't so fortunate....

Some time before I was old enough to hunt, Dad bought into a Potter County, Pennsylvania hunting camp. The county's slogan being: "God's Country: the Whitetail Capitol of the World." He hooked up with a bunch of Greensburg, Pennsylvania cronies; dear friends, most of them. There were the Morelli's, the Rosatti's, the DiPrimio's and, of course, the Parry's—the Americanized name for "Parisi." There were other Italians who were camp members and, it doesn't need said, spaghetti and meatballs were a sacred commodity in that camp! Ten (I think there were thirteen?) Italians in a deer camp has to be the next worse thing to ten clowns in a one-room schoolhouse. Indeed, Camp Lyman was a place forever etched in the mind of anyone who ever said grace at the Last-Supper-like table. Regardless, though, of how fun-loving Dad's gang of cronies was, they took their deer hunting as seriously as the Pope might hear confession.

As a boy of the fifties, it was the very bread of life to have something paramount to boast about. I always found things about Dad to brag on since there was so little in my accomplished repertoire even remotely boast-worthy. Jimmy's dad got a nice buck. Johnny Spitznogle's dad shot doubles on grouse. "Pinhead's" dad took a limit of squirrels with a Stevens single in .22 rimfire and Johnny Andrew's dad busted a tom turkey with an 8-inch beard! Etc., etc.! It got old pretty quickly and I was abusing the story about Dad's getting over eighty parking tickets in front of his own heating and plumbing shop in town. Even though he accomplished this in well under six months! The guys had heard it long enough and I'd already worn to mere gauze the stories of his prizefighting career. I desperately needed Dad to kill, finally, a braggable buck. It would've been the ultimate true-life tale, for in those days hunting was the thing and a man's prowess in the big woods of the whitetail was more commendable, at least to youngsters, than a chestful of war medals.

But, year after buck-less year went by and Dad, coldheartedly I felt, even quit getting parking tickets. And Dad to his dying days was one of the best rifle shots I've ever known. Still, never **once** did he bring home a deer from the Potter county camp. How well I can remember my nose, pressed hard against an icy, winter's window, awaiting Dad's arrival home from Camp Lyman, the place of my boyhood dreams. I'd get unbearable butterflies in my stomach just with the anticipation of seeing a buck strapped to the fender of Dad's old Ranch Wagon but, there never was. . .

I think I was fourteen when Dad invited me along on the sacred, annual ritual, the trip for deer to Camp Lyman. Five glorious days of playing "hooky" with full permission! There seemed to be something keenly celestial about the whole idea. I thought of how often I played hooky without rhyme or reason and now, in an abstract sense, it was "legal." I was going in an attempt to supplement the family's winter larder with venison. In a way, I felt, earning my "bacon."

**Camp Lyman:** The broken screen door had no apparent function or value insofar as keeping anything out. The main door, too, was all but worthless and had to be lifted and shoved simultaneously in order to get it to open and,

169

even though we locked it when no one was there, the lock was fraudulent, nothing more than a hardware façade. It didn't "lock" out anything. . .

There were bunk beds in two bedrooms, a total of six sets, and each had a ticking that always appeared somewhat aggressive looking to me. There, too, were enough mouse droppings on each to effectively fertilize at least several gardens. A wood cookstove in the corner of the main room could easily have been owned by Methuselah himself. And **he** may very well have considered it an antique! There wasn't any running water, at least inside camp, but some 100-yards away was a spring, to where buckets were carried (I was official spring boy once I became part of the gang!) when water was needed. And, of course, the hallowed outhouse! A place forever supplied with several Sears' catalogs, most of which had only those shiny, terribly slippery, awful pages remaining; the good ones with no slickiness were always gone—hidden somewhere? The sofa was unsightly, almost formidable looking with its springs poking out here and there. As though the Chinese army had used it for target practice on one of their better days.

And the one upholstered chair? It was one of those overstuffed recliners the size of Rhode Island with bulging springs that looked as though "they" had homicidal inclinations. I soon came to learn it was not as comfortable as the sagging hardwood floor and, for a time after the first visit, I had butt scars to prove it.

And yes, the all-important main table. It was massive and surely the reason for the demise of several large trees? Not level, certainly, and so far from it that once during a spaghetti and meatball dinner, Uncle Danny removed his glass eye when I wasn't looking and set it next to his plate. Soon, the creepy little thing rolled clear over to my side of the table, ultimately stopping by the side of **my plate!** And there it lay. Motionless and staring right up at me as though I'd done something wrong—or it wanted something and I was unable to provide it? I never, until that vivid moment, knew Uncle Danny had a glass eye! But, at the time, the whole table of hunting Italians roared with laughter as I sat there in a staredown with that part of Uncle Danny I wish (to this day!) I'd never come to know! I ate all of my pasta, but needless to say, the meatballs went unscathed; I would save them for another, less traumatic time. . .

I think the Camp Lyman gang put 8 deer on the lodgepole that year? None of which were mine—or Dad's. I do recall clearly, coming back to camp for lunch two days in a row, and finding Dad fast asleep on the vindictive sofa. I also recall one of the guys asking him about whether he'd seen the buck "that surely" went past his early-morning stand. It was, according to the account, "the nice little buck that was running with a group of does, one of which was a rare piebald." Dad denied seeing the buck, but as his son, I detected something in his tone and expressive eyes that told me something different. "Why though," I thought, "would Dad lie about something like that?"

How well I can summon the memory of a queasy stomach when I suspected Dad of lying about **not** seeing the buck. I never, however, questioned him, feeling his reasons may have been private and I was always taught to fully respect a man's privacy as well as his **need** for it.

Several more deer seasons came and went and I'd killed my fair share of whitetails, but Dad? Dad went without killing one for some eighteen years. Still, in my heart, I was unable to "call up" the courage to ask, "Why, Dad?" He could shoot and everyone who knew him also knew he could make a rifle "talk." He used to shoot out the bullet holes in our paper-plate targets and the law of averages, in those days, was surely on his side? There were a lot of deer, especially in Potter County, and Dad had one of the choice stands in the area we hunted near and around old Camp Lyman. Still, he left Pennsylvania back in '59 and moved with our family to the San Diego area, never killing a Pennsylvania whitetail. Lost to a sort of "retirement," was one of the best rifle shots the Lyman gang ever had. . .

Back in 1990, a long time after this story took place, I'd moved my family west, to eastern Oregon's Baker City in the Powder River Valley. We've since returned to Pennsylvania, but while there in Baker, Pap and my stepmother came for a visit (we came to call him "Pap" in his later years.) It was about three years before I would lose Pap forever and it hurts to even type that. Of course, I didn't know that then.

As he sat near the woodstove in our living room, warming himself, I felt I'd ask him for the long-needed answer. I didn't want to; I just seemed to have this inner-need that was more powerful than my will power. And so, I asked.

"Pap, you were one of the best rifle shots in the county, and I know, a fine hunter in those days of Camp Lyman and Potter County. Why you used to make the nearly impossible shots on cottontails and some on ringnecks I feel ought to go down in history!" I was smiling at him then. "Why no deer Pap? In all those years when you were on top of your shooting game, not one deer? Why, Pap?" I smiled again as I awaited the answer.

He sat there for what seemed an hour, his head down as he tapped gently on my foot with his cane. Finally he looked up at me, his cheeks wet with but two tears, and looking as warmly into my eyes as he ever had. Then through the heart of a war veteran came, "Hell, Joey. I don't know. I guess I was good on rabbits and ringnecks because not one of them ever looked me in the eyes. . ."

And, finally, I understood. As best I could anyway. Not all war veterans make good deer hunters—and vice-versa.

That was the last time I spoke with Pap in person. The last time I saw him alive. He finally succumbed to another "war" inside of him. And I've since tried to console myself with a certain knowledge. Pap got his satisfaction with and from, life. And none from death. No doubt the reason his eighteen buck tags went unfilled?

And, you know, I'd give most anything to talk with him. Just once more. I'd tell him it was okay that he never killed a whitetailed buck for me when I was a kid and that he's still my hero. Forever and regardless, Pap. . .

Dedicated To:
Frank Joseph Parry, "Pap"
June 21, 1920-June 22, 1994
159th Engineer Combat Battalion Corporal

AUTHOR'S NOTE: I could not say what I needed in this introduction even nearly as well as a wise Native American, Big Thunder, of the Wabanaki Alogonquins. The story will clear understanding as to why I chose the words of my brother, Big Thunder who said "The Great Spirit is in all things; he is in the air we breathe. The Great Spirit is our Father, but the earth is our mother. She nourishes us; that which we put into the ground, she returns to us…"

So it is written, and so it is true? I have proven this time and time again, but still await Daniel.


## "Of A Predatory Heart"


A Hunter of forty-plus years sits; the smoke from a meditative pipe curls like a bland wreath about his graying head. He is in ever-deepening thought. Outside, it is deadly, bitter cold. The earth around his forest home is smothered by a half-fathom of snow. So cold, this night, the crystals of snow appear like so many strewn diamonds and the silvery, full moon somehow, by some celestial magic, casts a lambent glow onto the blanket of white, making it appear strangely bluish. And, at this he wonders, saying to himself, "God at work in his most favored art studio…"

He continues to think, this time more deeply. Becoming more intimate with his heart's language, his mind's hard-earned wisdom, he gazes through the window. The snowy diamonds glitter, seeming almost alive and cosmic as he trips the switch to the front yard floods. They flicker magically under the cast light of the full moon and that which he has added. "This world has given me riches far more precious than jewels." He thinks aloud, though whispering now, as he falls into a more melancholy frame of mind. The floods are shut off and the moonlight allows that virtually none of the beauty of this harsh winter's night is lost. Instead, it becomes even more beautiful to him, for now it is all natural. Alone, the work of his Heavenly Maker, and to himself, he smiles...

He knows his time has come, for he fought it off for some time now, this ever-stronger feeling in the depths of his heart. He sighs, knowing his thinking of being alone with his thoughts, is about to steal away something very dear to him. Something some say, "He lived for his whole life long..." He walks away from the window with a cumbrous heart for somehow, he is torn by his tentative decision. But he knows. His heart knows as does his ageing mind, that he is fast-losing his sedulous desire, his ancient, atavistic instinct, his natural God-given need to kill. He wants so, to hold on, if just for one more season of him against the elements, against the alleged odds, against the magically elusive whitetails he so loves. All of these he seemed forever able to defeat and conquer, regardless of the pains and frustration they sometimes caused. But it was time. His heart had spoken and he always followed its commands and, holding on emotionally or otherwise, would be but a superficial feeling.

The tea-kettle whistles to him from the kitchen. His deerskin moccasins allow him to slip quietly across the room so as not to awaken his two sleeping children, his wife of nearly a quarter-century. He thinks of his beloved native American brothers and how they might describe his silent walk: "Like a shadow of a cloud passing across a field..." But he has always been respectful of their need for rest, for time alone, for space, freedom, and quiet. As he has always been with the whitetails, the second love of his predatory life.

Above all things at which he excels which may be a precious few, deer hunting is what he does best, save loving his family who so tolerantly put up with his passions for the hunts of Autumn; of his love for guns and gun powders and bullets and shooting and yes, perfection in utilizing them all...

The well-sugared tea warms him, affords his body and degenerative back added life, if just for the shortest time. Again he fights the urging in his heart, and whispers to his own, half-deaf ears, "I don't think I can hang it up." He wonders about what he will do to support his family. What he will do to fill his heart come autumn? He, after all, is by profession, an outdoor writer; a man who, for years heard the friendly-fire joking of his readership who referred to him as, "The Whitetail Man." How will he write of deer hunting if he follows his heart? For this is what helped, substantially, in his gaining an unassuming reputation as a writer of whitetail hunts...

He thinks, "I cannot write of current affairs for they for the most part, depress and flood despair upon the readers. I cannot write of professional football, for it is violent and there's enough of that in God's world. And too, it is too much like big-business with the titanic salaries and the players are but huge, fleshly facades that have little love of the sport, though there are exceptions.

"I cannot, certainly, write of society for it is that which I have for all my adult years, tried so to escape or at worst, avoid. What then will I do if I choose not to hunt the whitetails, the animals I most love and best know?"

The time is 3:15 A.M., and the night deepens into something almost celestial, almost holy perhaps? Another cup of steaming, revitalizing tea warms his palms as he stares through the window. It is beautiful and the drifts of snow appear to him as white waves on an albino sea that God has frozen before they could break and flow to shore. Almost inviting they seem, even with the deadly cold revealed on the thermometer as minus one degree. There is no wind. The spruce outside his window stands dead-still, frozen and in dormant sleep.

An aging set of snowshoes hang upon his makeshift office wall next to a photo of a writer friend, Charley

Waterman. Charley smiles, seemingly beckoning him as he stares at the photo, challenging him to, "Go, Joe, go!"

"Crazy," he thinks aloud, "too late and far too cold." But then he remembers of his last hunt, the first day of antlerless deer season. He looks down at the finger of his right hand, a painful reminder that was severely stung, frostbitten, by yet another day of deadly, Arctic-like cold. "The sacrifice," he says to himself, "I forgot to offer my sacrifice after I killed the doe!"-He, a man who deplores the proverbial, "loose ends."

His thoughts drift to a time nearly thirty-years ago, when he'd spent a summer on the Wind River Reservation in Wyoming. There he learned the ways of the people he most loves, the Native Americans. They taught him the ways of the hunter, a brave, the "Indians'" ways, all of which are good. "You must always make your sacrifice to Mother Earth when she gives to you, Joseph Lone Eagle, or she will not yield you anything more, ever…"

They called him, after he became blood brother to one chief, Joseph Lone Eagle, because of his constant need for time alone. When fishing, hunting, when just exploring along the banks of the Wind River, his blood brother, perceptive as most of the Native American people, noticed his displeasure when anyone would try to follow him, talk with him, or even watch him as he headed out to those wild places beyond sight of Crowheart, the small town where he'd stayed while visiting the Shoshones, the Arapahos.

He recalled clearly, accurately, the words of his blood brother: "You Joseph, are a man who starves for solitude, time to gather yourself and your inner-spirit into one being. Your mind into a single thought mass. Your heart wants always to be open to one feeling at a time, so it may fully taste of it and, so, in the tradition of the Shoshones, I shall name you Joseph Lone Eagle, for you have also, many times, told me of your love for that great hunter of the sky. Of your envy of his unbound freedom. It is fine with your brother that you feel this way. I understand your need for being alone. It is a manly thing to crave solitude if he is to be worthy of his title, man. A man cannot touch his dreams or reach out to them, nor speak to his heart and listen to it without quiet time alone. And so it is with you. Perhaps, more so than most, for you are a writer, a deep thinker and a loner in disguise. I see how you show love for your fellow man, but when you are done with it, you again wish deeply for solitude, that which your eagle heart most craves. Yes, you are, from this day on, Joseph Lone Eagle. I shall tell this to the others, so that they will know of and respect your need."

He laces on his boots, the unmade sacrifice being his motivation, and swings a goose-down jacket around his shoulders. The snowshoes are taken from their mooring and carried to the steps of his porch. Snowshoes secured, he steps down onto the crusted snow, being strangely careful so as not to trample those crystals that look to him, like diamonds, so many cosmic jewels. He will travel the long mile, perhaps more, to the spot where his last whitetail was felled, a doe on the run. The full moon would make for his easy navigation; his favorite pipe would warm his cotton-gloved hands.

The night seemed without life, but he is a hunter. He knows better. There are a thousand eyes watching his every move; a thousand sentient ears listening intently to every step and breath he takes. A screech owl brings his mind back to reality and he smiles with frozen cheeks: "Good morning." He whispers to the owl, unseen but somewhere near and above his cowered head. He is glad to have the company, however short the time...

His snowshoes barely mar the crusted snow and the going is easy, though the distance greater than he'd anticipated. Or is it his aging, degenerative back stretching the distance? No matter now.

The hollow looks alien to him in the moonlight. The shadows stretching out like so many more trees lying upon the ground where, before, there were none. The sterile whiteness of this always enchanting belly on the earth makes it appear more vast, more desolate and lonely. Like that of the lunar surface. He feels a bit lost but to him this is good.

178

"It is good to feel this way, for it stirs the adrenalin and pits it against the steely cold, warms my aching bones..." At least this is what he thinks, for he knows it helps him, psychologically to ward off the grave discomfort of the night's bitter cold.

He hears the near-silent whisper of a great horned owl's wing beats in a desperate, perhaps futile, stoop toward something unknown to him, unseen. He smiles and speaks. "Hunt on comrade, for I too, hunt. But in the light of day and with far more advantage than that which God has given you." He feels it is healthy to talk to oneself, to the wildlife that crosses his chosen paths. For wild things talk back without words, to his mind, the same as being in agreement with him. He laughs as he thinks, "Perhaps I should have wed a great horned owl?"

Two more hollows and he should be there. There on the hogback where he killed the white-tailed doe and yes, there where the bitter cold froze his four-pound gray mass, his brain, causing him to forget the tradition of sacrifice taught to him by his beloved Shoshone brothers. There, in the place that may very well lay claim to his frostbitten finger which, on this night, ached as though it were being steeped in the juices of Hell. A small price, he feels, for all the pleasures, all the inspiration, all the winter venison so cherished by him and his family. And, of course, all the other joys bestowed upon him in those yesterdays he forever revisits that dwell within his heart. He thinks of the possibility of his finger being lost: "I have lost far more in my associations with unkind mortals, and those scars do not show. And time indeed, does not heal all wounds..."

He laughs again as he thinks of his wife, of her probable enjoyment of his frozen jaws- his not being able to speak a permanent thing. Whitetails and family—always on his mind...

One more hollow, he wonders? For the time has been longer than he thought it should. He sits and rolls the warm, briar bowl of his pipe about his cold cheeks. "Is my sense of time and direction degenerating too?" No, it's not, as he

179

looks back over his shoulder and spots the hogback upon which his deer had fallen in an instant death. "Finally." He whispers...

He attempts to build a small, hand-warming fire with tinder he chips from the ragged, dry bark of a hickory and fallen boughs from a hemlock. There is no breeze to aid the cause and his hands are rigid with the ever-deepening cold. He trembles until, finally, the small fire begins to warm him.

From his pocket, he removes a photo of a most beloved and recently fallen friend. He whispers, "Hello, Daniel Loud." It is the only photo he has of his longtime friend who passed on but days before; a hurtful blow even to the so-called, calloused hunter, the predator of God's making, whose hunts are dictated by the heart.

His memory serves him dutifully of hunts past with this man, this friend of but a few in his lifetime. And so with this store of memories, he feels that the photo is not all he has left of his fallen friend, still, it is precious to him...

He folds the photo into a tiny square and whispers, "Until we meet again, my friend." And with that, he buries it in the litter of the forest floor then covers it with lichen and pine needles-and over the top of it all, he sprinkles a goodly amount of his most favored pipe tobacco. He looks skyward into the pastel blue of early dawn: "This," he whispers, "is all I have to give as physical sacrifice, but one day there will be more, and soon..."

He stands to leave as the soft, blue sky brightens, showing a sliver of lucent sun. Walking toward home, his thoughts become mosaic-like, a mixture of something lost, something gained. Oddly enough, he is cold no more and the light of morning seemingly shortens his return home.

His wife awaits him, watching from a window as he struggles over the crusted snow on the large field before their home. She waves to him, but at that moment he couldn't see through his flooded eyes. He blinks to clear his sight and sees her stepping onto the front porch deck.

"Well, Old Man of the forest, where have you been?"

He looks up at her as she holds open the front door, forces a smile from the depths of his heart and says, "Church. I've been to church."

"And the sermon?" His wife questions.

He sits on the step for a moment and in his eyes there's a look she has never before seen. "Well?" she asks.

"The sermon?" He says, his voice weakened, hindered by a stabbing in his throat. "The sermon was about sacrifice. About man learning how and when to recognize that time when he must move over for a new generation and about the self-mandated cessation of beloved quests in his life, whether one or many. And there was talk of pursuing new dreams, you know? Narrowing it all down to but a single dream? Like my lifelong dream of killing one, giant, whitetailed buck?"

And sure she knows. She's been his wife nearly twenty-five years. His wife who has, for so long, been tolerant of his crazy dreams and hunting passions. She places her hand on his shoulder and he looks at her through grateful eyes and speaks. "You know, even as the earth sleeps beneath the strain and cold of snow, the animals of the forest struggle. So tenaciously they hang in there, determined to survive, to find their next meal, especially the whitetails. How I love them for the many years of joy, of sometimes grueling challenge in fair chase and those many times they let me win. It is time to close a certain chamber of my predatory heart forever and only leave open that one which has yet to fill. Do you understand what I'm trying to say?"

Softly, she answers, "Yes, of course I do. I thought this would happen to you years ago."

He rubs his weary eyes, his aging, weathered cheeks wrinkle to form the slightest smile. "Remember the time I told you of a summer I'd spent with the Indians and how they named me Joseph Lone Eagle?" He doesn't await an answer. "And how they taught me the ways of the Indian hunters and the sacrifice that must always be part of the hunt? That if man, as a hunter takes from Mother Earth, he must always put something back, something of personal value?"

"Yes." His wife whispers, her arm now warming his shoulder.

"I did that today in the hollow where I killed the doe. I gave tobacco, my cherished photo of Daniel and my solemn promise during the offering. I promised to move over, to allow the young hunters their sacred bounty and I gave thanks for the many years of joy I've had hunting the whitetailed doe .I didn't do this without considerable reservation, but I've given my word and will forever hold to my promises. From this day forward," he looks into her eyes and smiles, "Joseph Lone Eagle will hunt only the majestic, giant bucks that have haunted his dreams in each of his forty-years a hunter."

A sort of pellicle now covers a very special chamber of his predatory heart. It seals well, the promises he made in the enchanted hollow of the whitetailed doe and, in that this writer knows him intimately, it is certain to forever remain, just that way…a promise well-sealed.

"Come into the house," said his wife, "You must be awfully tired?"

"No," he said, "No, I'm not so tired. Just cold. Very, very cold." Already he was missing his only photo of his dear, dear friend, Daniel…

And yes, he feels a hurt, a sense of great loss. For no longer will he hunt the whitetailed doe, no longer can he hunt with his fallen friend, at least on Earth. But he is a hunter, a predator of God's miraculous making and he had, so very long ago, learned to live with life, with death and, with sacrifices. It is all too familiar to his predatory heart…

"Babbling Tonic"

I took my rod and heavy heart,
Down to the stream one day,
Not so bent on catching trout,
But to watch the crayfish play...

I sat tired above an eddy,
Near a pool, cool deep and clear,
Watching crayfish swimming up, then down,
In their comical reverse "gear."

I wondered about a city life,
Where countless millions just have to dream,
Of sitting in the calm of woods,
On the banks of pristine streams...

I felt some sorrow, just for them,
While sitting within my "cure."
And knowing I'm a fortunate soul,
With this serenity near my door.

Then home I went with a lighter heart,
Whispering small prayers as I walked
Wishing I could share this gift from God,
This stream,
To which I've talked...